The Isle of
Mr Bengt's Wife
The Last Shot

August Strindberg

Translated from the Swedish, and with footnotes by
George W. Bramley

ISBN 979-8-8671-5622-0

The Isle of the Blessed

Chapter One

The three-master *Swedish Lion* had just hoisted its spritsail and the studding sail on the foremast as it stood in front of the fortress of Älvsborg, and was about to raise the anchor when one of the customs boats pushed off from land and signalled that the ship was not yet to set sail. But the wind had already filled the foresail and the ship was drifting at anchor. The customs boys rowed for all they were worth. The end of a rope was cast out, and soon the customs boat was being hauled up towards the great hull. Two young men climbed out of the boat and slipped through a cannon port in the side of the vessel. A leather sack was thrown after them, which appeared to be their only luggage, and then the customs boat set off again. But the *Swedish Lion*, which by now had lifted its anchor up over the cathead, put gently to sea to the steady accompaniment of the starboard cannons, which were answered in kind from the fortress.

The *Swedish Lion* was laden with forgings, clothing and cargo - as well as some five hundred passengers, consisting chiefly of criminals drawn from anchor smithies, prisons and penitentiaries. Its destination was the colony of New Sweden in North America.

As soon as the young men had made their way up through the lower quarters and were standing on deck, they turned round and, seized by the same thought, both stuck out their tongue. It was difficult to tell whether this gesture was directed at the fortress or at the country in general, which was now drifting away into the blue behind them. After thus expressing their patriotic sentiments, they went to seek out the captain's cabin in the stern castle in order to present their papers and offer up an explanation.

From the account they now gave it came to light that they were students of the Uppsala Dominus Academy, Lasse Hulling and Peter Snagg. Both had been convicted of giving a deprecatory speech, in the city's vaults as well as a provincial commercial concern, in which they criticised the recently published secular work *Atlantis* or *Manhem* by the King's Professor Serenissimus Olaus Rudbeckius,[1] who had elevated the honour of the fatherland in a hitherto unimagined and inconceivable manner by making the assertion, backed up by a comprehensive body of evidence, that the Kingdom of Svea[2] was nothing less than the cradle of humanity. For giving a foolish and discourteous speech in which they had expressed their doubts about this, Hulling and Snagg had been placed in an institution of detention, but since their conduct in this cramped and unhealthy domicile was inappropriate and culpable, they had been sentenced to running the gauntlet and penitentiaries.

Pardoned by His Highly Merciful Majesty the King, they had been granted permission to flee the kingdom and on the *Swedish Lion* to travel to New Sweden.

The captain accepted the explanation with a broad smile. He had not heard of the book *Atlantica,* but when he learned that it had something to do with the idea that the Kingdom of Svea might have been the sunken Atlantis or

---

[1] An exaggerated but humorous reference to the Swedish practice, common at the time the work was written, of using Latin names for important or distinguished persons, e.g. King Gustavus Adolphus.

[2] The name of an early tribe that ruled much of the present-day territory of Sweden and which gave the country its name.

the Isles of the Blessed, he immediately warmed to the students' story and explained that every seaman was aware that Atlantica lay in the Great Ocean, or the Atlantic Ocean, which had acquired its name from these very islands. He then bade both gentlemen welcome and they became good friends.

The journey progressed with fair winds across the North Sea, through the English Channel and out into the Bay of Biscay. Since, in the event of a shipwreck, it was too great a risk to have the captives tied and, in any case, there was no fear of escape or mutiny as everyone had declared themselves willing to travel, they were free to walk and they conducted themselves sensibly and decently. The married ones were reunited with their wives and children, whom they had not seen for many years, and they were blissfully happy and their happiness made them good. Not that they had been all that bad to start with. Some had pulled a knife while drunk, others had evaded military service, while still others had picked fruit from other people's trees as they had none of their own. Having been dragged out of dark, unhealthy prisons, they delighted in the sight of the great ocean, which bathed them in light. Everything was new to them and they played on the deck like children. Now they would see a dolphin dancing on a wave, now they would watch how one of the seamen caught a shark or a flying fish.

Released from their labours, they experienced the entire journey as a holiday, and they would sit at a modest but ample, clothed dining table without any worries about their upkeep.

The two students, who had once had the rope around their necks but had somehow got away, felt they were in some way accomplices, and they struck up an acquaintance with those who had been liberated and who, like them, were to start life's struggle afresh in a new country and in new conditions. As a consequence of his nature and upbringing, Lasse's view of the world was that everything happened for the best. Peter, on the other hand, was of the opinion that everything was beyond redemption. The two friends would often find themselves arguing over these two versions of life philosophy and, in so doing, each attracted his own adherents. The ship's doctor settled the dispute by declaring both of them correct. Life is both black and white, he said. He who only sees the black side sees black in everything; he who only sees the white side thinks everything is white. That's just how it is.

They landed on the nine isles of the Azores, where they were allowed to go ashore and stretch their legs. They thought they had come to Paradise as here they found vines, maize, oranges, pineapples and melons growing under the open sky. A cut-throat, who had spent six years in an anchor smithy, was so ecstatic that he had to be tied down, and he lay bound by a stream eating orange after orange until his face turned yellow around the nose. He was convinced he was Adam, and would strip naked, wearing only a tobacco leaf. The ship's priest took him by the hand and explained that it was sinful to go around unclothed, but the man proved, on the basis of the Holy Scripture and the Bible story, that after committing his sin, Adam wore only a fig leaf, and he therefore considered it his right to go around in a tobacco leaf. The priest, however, demonstrated on the basis of the church fathers and the *Flora Exotica Sacra* that a fig leaf was not a tobacco leaf.

The passengers were eventually led back on board. They set sail and made for Antigua. The journey had hitherto gone smoothly and well, apart from a minor storm in the North Sea. But now, as they were about to enter the horse latitudes, they found themselves in the doldrums. All around them lay the sea like a dead horizon of mercury, on which the ship moved like a magnetic needle. The heat became unbearable, tar oozed from all of the stacked merchandise and from the joints in the hull. They spent a whole day dousing the ship, afraid it would catch fire. This continued for eight days.

Then, early one morning, the look-out on the foremast announced that he could see some clouds to the north. The captain, who knew what this meant, had the cannons and everything loose secured and the hatches fastened immediately, and told everyone to prepare for the worst. After several hours, at breakfast, a black streak could be discerned on the horizon. A few hours later they could hear a rumble, like waves breaking on the shore, or the roar of traffic in the city; and the storm began its onslaught over the waters. Yards, spars and tops had all gone over board before the sails could steer the vessel, and on course sails alone the *Swedish Lion* drifted onwards towards the south, without anyone knowing where she was heading.

The storm raged for three days, and they expected the keel to strike against the sea bed at any moment. The priest read and preached, and stated that nothing else could be expected as there were so many criminals on board. He reminded people of Jonas, and suggested to the captain that all the criminals should be thrown overboard in order to save the righteous, as instructed by the Prophet Micah, Chapter XII, Verse 16 and what followed, but the captain refused. When the danger was at its greatest, Lasse Hulling approached the priest and proposed that a service of common prayer and scriptures should be arranged straightaway, since, he said, it is only unrepented crimes that put things on an uneven keel. The proposal was accepted, and the confession, from which the criminals were excused as they had already confessed their crimes, commenced.

From the investigation carried out, not one righteous person was found. But the storm raged on. Then a faint murmuring could be heard from below deck in the forward hold. People had been thinking things over, and some bright spark had the idea that the priest should confess too, as he was the only one who had not confessed his sins. The proposal was met with acclamation, but they still had to find a suitable father.

In the end, Peter Snagg put himself forward as he had attempted to study Hebrew for his priest's examination. The priest protested, but in vain. They bound him to the main mast, and after harsh remonstrances as well as friendly admonitions he finally confessed, in a flood of tears, that he had once seduced a child of the Eucharist in his youth.

There then followed a consultation, in which the passengers also participated, and whilst the priest elected for throwing all five hundred of them overboard, it was soon decided that the priest was the one who should be thrown into the sea, as instructed by the Prophet Micah, Chapter XII, Verse 16 and what followed. After saying his final prayer, he was cast into the ocean.

But the storm was increasing all the time. Finally, at middle-watch on the seventh day the ship ran aground. A loud cry answered the thud of the hull as its prow ran up against an underwater rock, so that it now stood on end. The cannons came loose from their lashings and crashed down through the lower decks. The ship began to go down as day was dawning. But suddenly, to windward, they sighted land.

Most of them managed to scramble into the life boats, but without taking with them the least provisions, or clothes or tools. When the sun rose, the boats had reached land, and all of them stepped ashore, one after the other, as they watched the ship sink like a stone.

Chapter Two

After seven days of toil and sleeplessness the travellers were so exhausted they immediately lay down to sleep on the ground underneath the trees that stood alongside the beach. But Lasse Hulling left with the captain to reconnoitre.

Their first observation was that they had never seen such a wonderfully pleasant land. What struck them the most was that they found themselves in such a warm, tropical climate at such a northerly latitude (they were still a long way north of the equator), and they found it necessary to lose some of their clothes. They soon discovered that the reason for this was the volcano, which rose gently like a rampart against the north wind and at the same time provided underground heating, which transformed the island into a greenhouse. Everywhere they saw palm trees with dates and coconuts, berry-fruit trees, bananas or pisangs (a kind of orange), pineapples, figs, giant strawberries, melons, which were either bearing fruit now or soon would be. They were in no doubt that they were on an island. Streams trickled under the shady canopy of the tamarind tree, and in the red granite they found springs of ice-cold water, which surprised them as they knew the ground was volcanic.

Parrots, honeyeaters and toucans with red, green, yellow, blue and gold-coloured feathers flew around in the trees and sang so sweetly, quite unlike the other species they had seen in cages. But they were also the only animals they came across. Their wanderings took them under the shade of trees and over meadows full of flowers, stretching all the way to the beach. The heat became more and more intense, and they had to abandon one garment after another. Around midday they started to climb the volcano, which appeared to be inactive, and towards evening they were able to rest at the foot of it, with only a palm leaf as a cover. They felt safe from attack from both man and beast, as they were certain they were on an island that was free from all dangerous animals and people.

The following morning they came down to the place where they had come ashore, and found their travelling companions stretched out underneath the trees, well fed and half naked, and day-dreaming. Lasse, who was the most capable and competent of them all, was appointed chairman of the deliberations that were now being held. People thought the island was delightful beyond description, but they had to think of the future. The first question concerned accommodation, as winter was approaching. To this observation Lasse immediately replied that, according to his calculations, they were now in the middle of winter. Those who wanted to live in stuffy huts could feel free to go and fell some trees and remove the bark with their nails, since they were without any kind of tools. Those who preferred peace and quiet instead could content themselves with making a shelter underneath the trees. Their second concern was food. Lasse assured them that, from what he had seen on the trees and plants, there should be enough food here to last the whole year, as when one tree finished bearing fruit another one started. The third objection came from the women, who were afraid there would come a day when they would need to go around without any clothes on. Lasse drew their attention to the fact that, to start with, they were walking around half-naked now in the middle of winter, and so when the spring came they would need to walk around totally naked because of the heat, whether they wanted to or not.

Since they had been given assurances regarding lack of food, clothing, lodgings, fuel and water, there only remained the task of settling down. And this they did. But Lasse gave them one piece of advice; they should not stay in one spot but spread themselves out around the island. When they had occasion to come together he would call for them by blowing on a horn, which he would not find difficult to procure. Then they split up for the day, as Lasse had been appointed chief and as such had given a speech in which he invited them to eat, drink and be merry, for they had now come to one of the Isles of the Blessed, of that there could be no doubt, and his only wish was that he had Professor Rudbeck with him, so that he could force him to eat his *Atlantica*, leather binding and all.

At night they all found shelter underneath some foliage hanging from tree branches.

But the following morning Lasse called together his closest friends, the captain, Peter Snagg and the doctor. After they had made themselves some breakfast by shaking a date palm, Lasse raised a number of important questions, which would most certainly become issues in the future. The first question he asked of the doctor: would they be able to live without meat and salt? The doctor believed that, from what he had read in travel books, they would not be able to tolerate eating meat in such a hot climate and, as far as salt was concerned, the fruits contained so much salt that they would no longer need to eat it.

While they were deliberating over this they heard a cry from the bushes close by. A man was led out, pale as a corpse and with clear signs of poisoning. Under questioning it came to light that, driven by a craving for meat, he had killed a bird with a stone and had attempted to eat it, but was immediately overcome with nausea and colic. The doctor ordered him not to eat any more meat again, and on that note this important question was resolved.

The second question was raised by Peter Snagg and concerned the introduction of an official church service, a census and legal powers. He knew how evil people could be, and if all of these good-for-nothings were to pass their time without any occupation, they would soon see their society destroyed by unrest. He therefore proposed to review the church's handbook, a copy of which he had saved, together with a copy of the Statute Book.

Lasse objected that since all causes for dispute, for instance lack of food, clothes and accommodation, had been removed, crime itself would cease. Who would steal if he had quite enough food for the day and didn't need to go out looking for more? Who would commit murder when there was no cause for envy, since everyone was equally rich and equally powerful? Who would commit burglary when there were no houses to break into? Who would kill their children when all children could eat their fill and no one needed to fear becoming a burden on society? He wanted to examine the Statute Book and revise certain paragraphs, the most important ones.

Lasse opened up the Statute Book and read:

'Primo: The Code of the Law of the Land! We could easily cross that one out as we don't have any land owners. All in favour?'

'Yes,' replied those assembled.

'Secundo: The Code of the Law of Inheritance! What is there to inherit? A fig leaf or a coconut shell! Delete?'

'Yes,' the assembled had to reply.

'Tertio: The Code of the Law of Construction! "Section 1. How building plots should be laid out and property altered. Section 2. How plots should be developed!" Since nothing at all is going to be built or altered, we can cross that code out as well, can't we?'

'Yes,' the assembly replied.

'Quarto: The Church Code! Since we don't have a church, we'll delete that one too?'

'Yes,' the assembly replied.

'Quinto: The Criminal Code! That one goes without saying, after what I've said about stealing, burglary and murder once the causes have been removed.'

'Yes,' the assembly replied.

'Sexto: The Marriage Code! Is the assembly willing to defer this question until we gain experience of it in the future? Because marriage is tied in with property, and if there's no property there's no marriage.'

'Yes,' answered the assembly.

But Peter Snagg objected.

'So,' Lasse interrupted, 'we've deleted the entire statute book, only the covers are left! We'll give them to Peter Snagg as a keepsake, shall we?'

'Yes,' the assembly laughed, but Peter did not give in.

'Veto!' he shouted. 'How can a society function without laws?'

'Listen, Peter,' replied Lasse. 'Laws are made to remedy society's defects. A society that doesn't have any defects doesn't need any laws! Am I right?'

'You're right,' replied the assembly.

'But Peter Snagg,' Lasse continued, 'he'd rather have a defective society with laws than an ideal one without them.'

Now Peter started to speak.

'I'll leave aside the question on civil law, be that as it may, but a society can't exist without religion!'

'Alright,' said Lasse. 'You're right about that! We must have a religion! But let's consider whether the old religion is suitable for us in our new circumstances! Will the assembly lend me their ears a while?'

'Yes,' replied the assembly.

'I'll start at the beginning,' said Lasse, 'or with the fall of man. People went around naked in Paradise and didn't do any work. All was well. Then, in disobedience, they ate from the tree of knowledge and were expelled and sent around the world to work! Well then, we've re-found Paradise, but a paradise without any tree of knowledge. Thus we couldn't sin even if we really wanted to. And even if we did sin we could be neither driven out, as we've nowhere to go, nor forced to work, as we've nothing to work with. So the fall doesn't apply to us and can be of no relevance to our circumstances. Is this agreed?'

'Yes,' replied the assembly, scratching their heads, but the captain tore off his shirt and went down to the beach to bathe.

'So,' continued Lasse, 'as there's no tree of knowledge, there's no sin. As there's no sin, there's no need for repentance, and the entire doctrine is not valid. Is this accepted?'

'The demonstration is accepted,' said Peter, 'but man's innate need for religion cannot be eradicated.'

'Granted,' replied Lasse, 'but if the need to go to church and play organs were innate, then this need would be present in everyone. Well, the savages didn't have any such need, and so the need to sleep in churches, play organs, put up hymn numbers and hold collections can't be an innate need, but an acquired one. Good! What has been acquired can also be lost. I wonder if we'll ever lose the need to be verbally abused by a drunken priest, to give away our last cow, with the priest reading aloud over a dead body, etcetera, etcetera… I just wonder.'

The doctor followed the captain's example and went down to the beach.

'It's far too hot to talk theology,' he said.

'But what about the grace of God?' Peter objected. 'And holidays, and those sacred moments of blessed peace!'

'We wouldn't be able to give grace as we don't have an ordained priest.'

'But,' replied Peter, 'we can have one ordained.'

'No,' replied Lasse. 'For that we'd need a bishop, and we haven't got one. Besides, we haven't got any wine, as I haven't seen any vines.'

'As far as that is concerned,' objected Peter, who was already bathing in sweat, 'wine could be replaced by coconut milk, or pineapple juice or fig juice.'

'Impossible,' said Lasse. 'Then we'd have to falsify the text. Listen: Jesus told his disciples: "I am the vine and you are the branches". He didn't say: "I am the coconut tree and you are the nuts", or "I am the pineapple and you are the thorns", or "I am the fig and you are the leaves". If we start altering the text now, we'd have to alter all of it. Nor do we have any bread. So we'd have to take a pisang and a pineapple and change the wording to: "Take this pisang and eat it…"'

'No,' said Peter. 'Now it's getting too hot. I'm going for a swim, are you coming?'

'All right,' said Lasse, 'and let's leave the theology alone!'

And so they went for a swim.

Chapter 3

A year had passed. None of their fears had materialised. The winter was just as warm as the summer. The seasons differed from each other only in the variety of crops they produced, and Lasse had devised a calendar of their ripening times. This also removed all monotony from their diet, and left them in the best of health. Thus they had four seasons, each of three months' duration: Pisang, Breadfruit, Date and Coconut. With Pisang, or January-March, came pineapples and oranges; Breadfruit, April-June, brought giant strawberries and figs; with Date, July-September, they had peaches and cherries; and with Coconut, October-December, came apricots and mulberries. In addition, there were constant supplies of melons, pomegranates, corn, peas and beans, so that the menu was always new and with endless possibilities. Since no one worked and the heat was so strong, they could only eat a little. After the long period of eating mainly salted food on the ship, the fruits provided a long-term cure for scurvy, and the consumption of vegetables gradually became the norm. A few isolated attempts at eating meat were punished by stomach upsets. An old drunkard had found a way of making an intoxicating drink from fermenting coconut juice, but it made him so ill he never tried it again, nor did anyone else. With these simple foodstuffs passions became more moderate, and only friendly words were uttered. It was impossible for envy to develop as everyone lived well and nothing happened to disturb the peace. Anger and hatred disappeared, and 'it was far too hot for anyone to want to brawl,' as the captain put it. As they had become unaccustomed to wearing many clothes, which in any case were falling apart, they developed the habit of going around half-naked, and eventually both men and women wore nothing other than a skirt of finely plaited leaves. The children went around completely naked.

To pass the time, they invented recreational activities and ball games. They would go swimming, riding or for walks. The children in particular took great pleasure in climbing trees, a passion that soon turned into a skill. Lasse had also introduced four major festivals, one to mark each season. They greeted each new harvest time with unconcealed joy, as the pleasure of finding variety in their food was something that came naturally to them. They would get together and eat for a whole day. Men, women and children would dance around a huge pile of the gathered fruits, and the first fruits were offered up to the benign Provider, just as Cain and Abel had brought offerings to the Lord, and this was a custom that everyone, including Peter Snagg, found beautiful and biblical.

Peter Snagg had tried to establish a free church, and wanted to read out a sermon to them. But he found everything so perfect, and when he asked for authorities and military powers there was absolutely nowhere to apply them. And at confession no one could speak sincerely as they had no sins to confess.

Peace, tranquillity and harmony reigned over society. All harsh words ceased to be heard and people addressed each other by affectionate names. They rejoiced whenever a child was born, and would welcome it into society with songs and games. The child was a valuable gift of nature, without the secondary monetary value that was attached to it in the country of their parents. Nor was it seen as a burden or punishment. When a young man and a girl wanted to be friends and have children together they would inform Lasse, who would celebrate the happy event without entering the young couple in any register, or obliging them to make promises to obey one another, so that if the one wanted to eat figs and the other pisangs then no law could make them eat the same thing. Since there were no rooms to clean and no pots to wash, the wife did not need to be subservient to her husband. Separate beds and seating were redundant because there were no beds or seating, just a pile of leaves underneath a tree.

Everything was as free, simple and unconstrained as possible. The mothers had no need to watch over their daughters as they had no need to be afraid that their sons-in-law would take their daughters for money, or that their daughters would go off and have children, as having children was considered a great blessing, and so the girl's condition when she was with child was also considered to be 'blessed'. There was only one thing that disturbed the peace on this Isle of the Blessed. This was the memory of the past, which came to people in particular in their dreams, and they would wake up screaming. An old blacksmith often dreamed of the anchor smithy, and felt the prison guard wake him up with a kick in the side. A cooper, who had taken to stealing because he had too many children, dreamed at night that his children were crying out for bread, and when he awoke to see the sun shining on the trees that always bore fruit, he would cry for joy and fall on his knees, thanking God for all that was good. But then he would be seized by thoughts of the future, and could not be consoled. This was the demon of the otherwise contented society; the thought of the future.

When they saw how good their life was then, they dreaded to think how they could get it back again if some vessel, for example, were to come and take them away. On the other hand, not one of them had cause to be homesick, for they had left behind either the penitentiary or military service, and no one was missing those exactly. So the memory of the past and fear for the future were the phantoms that disturbed their blissful peace, and both Lasse and the doctor would often ponder over what might help them, but to no avail. But what they could not think of, fate did.

One day the blacksmith had gone for a walk in the woods to get some fresh air after a sleepless night. In a cleft in the cliffs he found a bush bearing blue berries, which he had never seen before. He gathered some in his fist and ate them. They were not particularly tasty, but he didn't seem to mind. And then he went home, or rather to the bush where he had made a heap of leaves for the night. There he found his wife. The blacksmith was in high spirits and talked a lot of nonsense.

'I think you've had a drop or two to drink,' said his wife, who could still remember the past.

'What do you mean?' replied the blacksmith, taken aback.

'Brandy,' said his wife, smacking her lips.

'Brandy? I've never heard of that. What is it?' asked the puzzled blacksmith.

'If you don't remember what that was, then you certainly won't remember doing time in Karlskrona!'

'Karlskrona? I've no idea what you're talking about, old girl!'

'Then you've lost your memory,' said the old girl.

That was precisely what the blacksmith had done, and hence it became clear what the discovery was. The doctor immediately set about picking the berries and handed them out to everyone, telling them they were a cure for sleeplessness, and everyone ate them, including the doctor. But Lasse dropped his berries on the ground. He thought you never know what you might learn from the past, and no one knows what the future might bring.

Chapter 4

It was now three years since they had come ashore. Lasse decided to venture further inland to take stock of what resources the island held for the future, and assess whether it would support the large population that had grown over the past two years. By paddling a small canoe upstream under the dense canopy of the banana trees, he had managed to travel a good number of miles. Tired from rowing, he stepped out of the boat and sat under a banana tree to eat his breakfast, after which he lay down to sleep.

He had not been dozing for many minutes before he was awakened by a rustling high up in the tree he had been lying under. He looked up and, sitting on a branch high up in the tree, he saw what he thought was an ape. With his long nails he was skinning bananas, which he then inserted into his mouth, concealed beneath a long beard. Lasse became uneasy as this was an unexpected enemy that would create havoc for them if it had company, which it most probably did. He decided to lure the ape towards him and either capture him or kill him with a stone. He went off to fetch the biggest, ripest melon he could find, and armed with this in one hand and a stone in the other, he climbed up the tree.

First, he started clicking his tongue. The ape listened and threw a banana at Lasse's head.

'Coco,' Lasse said, showing him the melon.

But instead of answering, the ape climbed further up the tree, all the way to the top, which swayed under the weight like a bow being drawn.

'Coco, come on down, boy.' Lasse persisted. 'I've got something nice for you.'

Coco did not come down, however, but retreated even further. Seething with rage, Lasse called out: 'Would you just do as you're told…'

These words seemed to have a strong effect on Coco. He scratched his nose against the bark and tears streamed down his beard. Lasse heard him sigh but kept himself at a safe distance.

'For crying out loud, will you just come down here and eat this melon!'

The ape appeared to be deeply moved by this outburst, and Lasse no less so when he heard a human voice from high up in the banana tree.

'Why, that's the very speech of my home country, my native land and my friends and… I don't think I can hold back these tears. The old Nordic tongue has never sounded so sweet in my ears, and my heart is filled like a pitcher full of milk and honey in the late summer sunshine!'

'Good Lord, I do believe it's Pastor Axonius,' Lasse exclaimed. The priest answered immediately. 'Oh, it's me all right.' The two countrymen fell into a long embrace, their hairy chests bathed in the priest's tears.

'How in heaven's name did you get here?' was Lasse's first question. 'Didn't we throw you overboard? Did some whale come and swallow you up and then spit you back out onto land?'

'I wasn't spat out onto land. I swam ashore.'

'Tell me all about it.' said Lasse.

The priest dried his tears with a pisang leaf and sat down on a stone. He started to relate his story.

'Well, now that you mention it, I only remember being thrown overboard as if in a distant dream. I don't recall the reason.'

'Oh, there was reason enough, *ratio sufficiens*, to quote Aristotle.'

'Who is Aristotle?' the priest asked.

Aha, Lasse thought, he's been eating the berries too! 'Just go on, never mind Aristotle,' said Lasse.

The priest continued. 'After swimming around for an interminable length of time, I remember feeling the bottom underneath my feet, and then I walked ashore onto an island similar to this one. After eating some berries and drinking some water, I lay down to sleep. When I awoke I felt an extraordinary calm and peace, such as I had never felt before. Nature was for me like an open book, and the link between creation and creator seemed to be so simple. It felt as if something shady was lurking in my past, but I didn't know what it was. My head was light and I wasn't weighed down by any deep reflections. In a happy frame of mind, which I had never experienced before, I walked further into the island. I hadn't gone very far before I saw a man kneeling before an icon of a god, to whom he was praying. Aha, I thought, I had come to a heathen country, as my thoughts were still sort of mixed up with the vague ideas of old. Beside myself with rage at seeing such a base creature that was capable of crawling before an image produced by the hand of man, I took a stone and knocked the icon down. You should have heard it then! The man cried out, tugging at his hair, and called me a heathen. When he calmed down I asked him what religion he followed. He replied that he followed the benign Nicene creed. As I wasn't familiar with this, I asked him to explain. It was the most stupid belief I had ever heard of. It had also been adopted by the great council at Nicaea with a majority of only four votes. I asked him to clarify what god they worshipped and whether there are more than one god. "No!" he answered, they worshipped the only true god. "Good," I replied, "then we both worship the same god. But what then did he have to do with the icon that was hanging on the gallows?" "That's the son of God!" "It's a poor god whose son allows himself to be hanged." I said. Then he replied that this was something I didn't understand. That much I readily conceded, but he expressed the hope that when the holy spirit took possession of my heart all would be well for me. "The holy spirit; so you have three gods?" He replied that the devil still had control over me, but all would be well when I escaped his clutches. "Aha! You have four gods! And if the devil is the first in the world to rule over me, then I would pray to follow him. If he (who ruled over me) had created the marvellous world in all its splendour, and if he were the world's first, then he'd be the one I'd worship." And I fell down on my face and prayed to the world's first. But then the man let out a cry and summoned together a whole group of his followers. They bound me hand and foot. Then they led me to an odd-looking house with a gallows on the roof. "Who lives here?" I asked. "God lives here, for this is the house of God," replied one of the black men, for they were all dressed in black. "Oh my God, the world's first," I called out, "let your thunder strike them down for their impertinence! You, who live high above the heavens and have the sun, the moon and the stars as your footstool, you're supposed to dwell in this hovel?" At this point the eldest of the black men came up to me and started to speak amicably. He said that the Nicene creed was the creed of benevolence, and he therefore wanted to show me benevolence. He asked me if I wanted to love a

Jew who had suffered and died for this belief. To this I replied no because, firstly, I didn't know any Jew and, secondly, I didn't want to love anyone other than God. Then he grew angry and told me to go to hell. As I thought that hell, according to his benign faith, was supposed to be a good place, I replied, "With pleasure!" – "What?" he exclaimed. "You want to go to hell?" "Certainly." I said. Then they led me into the house of God! A man was standing by the door with a collection box, asking for money. I asked him if he showed his god for money. Then a servant came up to me and struck me with a cane. I asked him to be gentle with me as I was about to be instructed in the faith of benevolence. They then led me up to a large painting. It depicted hell. At the top appeared a mean old man with a long beard, above him a dove, and at his feet a lamb. They were surrounded by a whole host of other idols with wings, and underneath them was hell. It didn't look at all appealing. A number of darker gods with tongs were pinching men, women and children in the most sensitive places and afterwards threw them onto a fire. "That's terrible." I said, and I was seized by a blind urge to turn all these unfortunate people away from their idolatry. "If this is the benign Nicene creed," I said, "and if this is what hell is like, then I've no desire to become a Nicene!" And then I fell on my knees and prayed for them. "Oh God, creator and sustainer of the world, look down into the hearts of these unfortunates and touch their hard, deluded minds…" But I didn't get any further before I was knocked over and carried out.

'The next day I was to be burned alive because I didn't want to believe in the Nicene faith. I politely asked the elder if there was in their benign faith a milder punishment for a crime like mine. They answered no. The fire was made and upon it were placed foul images of the world's first, who had horns on his head and stuck out his tongue, just imagine, such heathens! I was led up to the wooden stake. Chanting songs and holding up images of idols in front of me, they prepared me for my death. I had never believed there could exist such savage people in the islands of the ocean. Now the time had come and I thought it was the end for me.

'But then the sky clouded over, and out of the clouds a flash of lightning, several flashes, struck down upon the house of god, amongst the images of the idols. "Look, look!" I cried. "God is striking down his own house! Do you still believe he lives there!" The black men dispersed, I broke free and fled. On the beach I took a boat and put to sea, preferring to die by God's hand rather than at the hands of those heathens. And now here I am, appealing to you to join me on a quest to convert these heathens to the one true faith.'

Lasse had been listening intently to the priest's extraordinary account, but towards the end he fixed his eyes even more intently on the volcano, which in the distance had been emitting a faint cloud of smoke.

'Let's go home first and talk to our friends,' he said, 'before embarking on any crusades to convert.'

They walked down to the boat and rowed home to informed discussions on the different types of heathens and the origin of the delusions of mankind. When they arrived home the sky had already become darkened by smoke, and faint rumblings could be heard in the distance. Everyone felt uneasy and no one knew what to expect. No one paid any particular attention to the return of the priest as they had other things on their mind. All through the night they kept watch and prepared the boats, which they had been prudent enough to store away and keep in good condition.

The sky was crimson like fire, and those who climbed the trees to gather food could clearly see what they were doing in the glow from the volcano. All the next day they continued to fill the boats with water, fruits and leaves, to safeguard themselves against the impending risk of hunger and cold. The rumblings increased and the ground trembled. On the third day they heard peals of thunder and a cascade of red-hot molten lava gushed out of the volcano.

Now everyone rushed into the boats and, distressed, weeping and sighing, they set off from the Isle of the Blessed, where the all-giving nature had fed them and clothed them for three years, where they had lived in peace and happiness, knowing neither strife nor zeal, and which they now had to leave behind to face an unknown fate.

When they came out onto the sea the island began to sink. The trees bowed low under the water, their tops swaying in the waves. The low hills were gradually submerged; eventually the volcano's peak began to smoulder in the waves. Each time the sea splashed down into the crater, it spurted back up again in a cloud of steam, red from the glowing lava, blue from the burning sulphur, and green from the copper and other metals, which had dissolved in the almighty cauldron.

And so the Isle of the Blessed vanished before the eyes of the unfortunates, who now abandoned themselves to the wind and the waves to face death or perhaps something even worse.

Chapter 5

When our travellers finally caught sight of land after five days of drifting around at sea, they were completely exhausted by the cold. The new land that opened up before them appeared to be a mainland, or at least a very large island. When they came ashore their food supply had been depleted, and they threw themselves voraciously at a mass of mussels that had been washed up on the beach, and from this oily food source they gradually regained their body warmth. The country seemed to have a cooler climate, and of all the wonderful fruit trees from the Isle of the Blessed there was not a trace. There were forests of beech, oak, birch and, further up the mountain, pine and fir. Hungry as they were, they tried to eat the acorns from the beech and oak trees, but they were not very filling and also unpleasant to the taste. But they found hares, deer, wild geese and sheep running amongst the trees, and capercaillie and grouse rustling in the bushes. So they understood from the start that their diet here would consist of game and fish, and that they would have to make warm clothes for themselves from the furs of the animals if they were not to freeze to death.

Lasse convened a large meeting, and proposed the following plan of action.

On the first day all of them were to go down to the beach to feed on mussels and then look for caves and hollow trees to spend the night. But those who had found a cave or a hollow would have to go and fetch mussels and water for some of those who were busy making arrows to shoot animals with, as they wouldn't have the time for that. Similarly, the preparatory work for the arrow-making involved looking for sharp stones, which could be used as knives.

By nightfall they had done no more than collect the sharp stones, and they crawled into their hollows and caves, or under up-turned boats, to sleep. The following morning they applied themselves to the task of making arrows. Some of them tried throwing stones to kill a few animals, which they then skinned to make clothing for the younger children. On the third day, when a good number of bows had been made, the men set off to hunt, taking along some of the women who were not expecting or had no children to look after. By now this had become a desperate measure as the mussels that had been washed up by the last storm had all been eaten. The hunt did not produce any great results. A dispute had broken out between the priest and the blacksmith. They had both been chasing the same hare, and were arguing over who had killed it. It might well have ended in an exchange of blows had Lasse not stepped in between them and settled the matter, suggesting they should share the catch.

'Now the battle begins...' thought Lasse to himself, and the whole scene made quite a sombre impression on those present.

The animals had to be eaten raw, which people found distasteful. But food was now being offered to expectant women and all those who had been obliged to stay at home for the sake of the children and who now demanded to eat too. No one wanted to share, so Lasse again had to step in and exhort every man who was a father to children, born or unborn, to share his catch with the women. But it proved impossible to deal with the fathers; for during the three years on the Isle of the Blessed men and women had intermingled with each other with no concern for fatherhood. Arguments developed, and Lasse again had to come between them. He separated the men and the women into two groups, and asked each woman to choose a husband. Every woman then had to make a solemn promise not to associate with any other man as long as her husband provided her and her children with food and clothes. Everyone considered this very reasonable. But Peter Snagg, who always found reasons to object, asked what the husband should do if the woman was unfaithful. Lasse replied that his responsibility to provide for her would cease, that is to say, he would have the right to divorce her or to drive her away, as it was not nature's intention that the one should work to pay for the other's pleasures.

'And now we have marriage all over again.' Lasse thought to himself.

All of the half-grown children were allowed to make angling hooks from the bones of the consumed animals, and using plaited grass as rods, they could try their hand at some small-scale fishing.

So the young society strove to make a living for some time to come. Winter was harsh in the caves as they were still without fire.

When springtime came they were horrified to find that the game reserves had almost been depleted. They spent more and more time hunting in the forests, but were allowed to spend nights away from home, although dragging their quarry back required great effort. Disputes about the catches were becoming a regular occurrence, and the peace was disturbed. Then one day, when their society seemed to be on the verge of collapsing, Pastor Axonius returned to the town with the firestone they had been needing for so long. It was a piece of sulphuric pyrite. But he was jealous of his discovery. Lasse, who was the only one who still had his memories, had a talk with Axonius about the treasure. For a long time now they had seen how unhappy the people were; they were clearly tired from the laborious hunting, and everyone longed for the good old days, when no one had to work. Making alcohol was commonplace, and the urge to shirk work pervaded society like a sin. Lasse and Axonius, who already had enough on their plates devising improvements for producing bows, making clothes and settling disputes, had little time left over for hunting. For this reason they had to beg the others for their food, and the others were reluctant to part with any. The time had come for them to stop begging, to demand to be fed and clothed as a service, in return for all their services to society. Winter was approaching, and the need for fire was felt more keenly than ever.

Lasse called everyone together. He explained it would be necessary to go off in different directions to look for new hunting grounds. They could only do this by taking their homes with them, as there was no certainty they would find caves every night. Living in transportable tents would solve the problem. But to live in tents you needed fire. The man who could start a fire whenever he wanted would be a genius. The gods of nature had given Pastor Axonius a greater insight into the secrets of nature than any of the others, and by using the pastor's knowledge, Lasse had devised a means of making fire. He now asked the people whether they would bring him and the priest food in exchange for firestones.

The assembly replied with a resounding 'yes'.

Lasse wanted to make a bonfire. He threw a raccoon skin over the priest's head and a fox skin over his shoulders. Then he turned towards the sun, addressing it as the source of fire, and muttered some words in Hebrew, to which the priest responded with an utterance that was just as incomprehensible. He then ordered the people to fall on their knees. The priest lit the fire and the flames were soon burning brightly.

'This is the beginning of a new era.' said Lasse. 'With fire we can go anywhere we like and never be short of game. *Hocus pocus, tantus talontus!!'*

And everyone danced around the beautiful fire in jubilation. But the priest, who had become the object of the people's prayers, hastily returned to his cave, where he hid himself away.

After making the people promise to bring regular tributes, Lasse handed out the firestones and ordered them to go off and make tents for themselves. They should then split up into five groups and each go their own way. They were to come back if they needed more firestones.

In seven days their their tents were ready, and they set off into the forests. They were instructed to return on a certain day of every year (except for when they came to pay their fire tax) at winter solstice when the days were starting to grow longer, gather as many people as possible around a great bonfire, and celebrate the return of the sun and the discovery of fire. Lasse also explained on behalf of Pastor Axonius that, in view of his intimate association with the gods, he would no longer have the honour of seeing them as often as before. He had also asked Lasse to announce that he would no longer be known by the name Axonius, but wanted simply to be called Bah, a word that carried great significance but the meaning of which was still not entirely clear to Lasse, as it was so profound it required six generations of men to fathom it out. And then they all went their own way.

But Lasse and Axonius, or Bah, as he was now called by a motion that did not need to be seconded, sat at home next to the fire and made a comfortable life for themselves. As they had more food than they could eat, they soon bribed some young men and women, who too had no desire to run around in the forests, to tend their fire, cook their food and sew their clothes.

'Now we've got masters and servants as well.' said Lasse to himself. 'I wonder how all this is going to end.'

Chapter 6

For some time Lasse lived in peace and contentment while receiving his tributes. But in the years that followed, the grand offerings dwindled and he soon found himself close to starvation. He sent out Bah as an inspector, dressed in a long robe made of body feathers, to terrorise the non-compliant into giving up their tributes. But for all his troubles, Bah was only given rough treatment and returned in tatters. People no longer believed in Lasse. Nor did they need his firestones any more since Peter had discovered where they could be found. But Lasse had something else up his sleeve, for he was a clever man and his memory was still intact. There was no longer any point in calling the tribes together, and instead he paid Peter Snagg and his tribe a visit. He wanted to strike him on his own ground in the presence of witnesses. Arriving at the Snagg camp town after a long and arduous journey, he went up to Peter and greeted him with respect. They had a conversation in private about a new invention, at the end of which they entered into a partnership. The tribe was assembled, and Snagg gave the following speech.

'Our life as hunters has not been without its trials and tribulations...' Sometimes there had been surpluses of meat, which just lay rotting, sometimes shortages. They had made some attempt to save the surplus meat by drying it, but had been let down by defective methods. However, Peter Snagg and Lasse Hulling had now found a secret stone that could keep meat, fish and hides from rotting. The possibilities of the greatest innovation of the era were incalculable. They would now be able to hunt at certain times and then relax, for relaxation was surely one of life's greatest pleasures. If the tribe were to pay Lasse and Peter their tribute now, they could have their invention.

This was answered with a thunderous 'yes'.

Peter handed out a white crushed rock, which he called salt, and invited everyone to come every week to collect their supply in return for leaving their tributes. And then Lasse returned home.

But the tributes were not very plentiful, as Captain Beard had already familiarised his tribe with a method of smoking meat, for which he received tributes himself, and Beard's men did not need any salt.

After the introduction of salt, people had more time to spare and became more settled. But they had grown accustomed to being constantly occupied, and now had the opportunity to think up new inventions. For example, Doctor Gadd, who received tributes from his tribe, had found a red metal that was very easy to pound and ideal for making arrows. This metal was, of course, copper, and its introduction made hunting a lot easier. It was also used for making knives and axes for felling trees. Now copper was sought everywhere but could not be found. The other tribes despatched messengers to the doctor, asking for details of the location of copper deposits. But he refused to divulge the secret, and instead sold knives and arrow heads in return for salt and firestones, of which he was in short supply. But his persistently high prices angered the other tribes, until one day Nipper the blacksmith, also a tribe leader, broke into his home and held the doctor hostage, along with his tribe. The doctor and his people pleaded for their lives, which they would be spared if they agreed to work for the blacksmith and his people, or became their slaves.

Alarmed by the danger, Lasse, who too was envious of the captain and the blacksmith, went out to look for a new metal that was sharper than copper and didn't bend when it was struck. With his iron picks and axes he armed his tribe, who now captured the captain's and the blacksmith's tribes. Lasse now had more on his plate than he ever imagined in his worst dreams, for it was difficult to feed and govern so many people all at the same time. There was also far less hunting now. He would have to start thinking of new sources of food, which could be kept close at hand and not chased in the forests. He instructed his people to catch aurochs, sheep and goats, which were tied to trees out in the meadows, and whose milk and meat could be taken on demand. He now had herdsmen under his command. It would be necessary to feed the animals over the winter and, for this purpose, create pastures, build barns and gather hay.

But people soon grew tired of the monotonous food, and old memories of the Isle of the Blessed resurfaced via their stomachs. Lasse used his time profitably. He discovered a couple of grass types with seeds that could be crushed and kneaded with milk to make a tasty dish. He had also found some plants with thick roots, which tasted bitter if they were grown in sparse soil, but sweet if the soil was rich. But he had no ploughs or bridled draught animals. He had the forests felled and burned, and in the ashes he sowed his grass and turnip seeds, and this gave rise to agriculture. Not all the tribes were keen to follow his example. But some did. With the felling and burning of the forests, however, the game disappeared. There were complaints about the dangerous smoke from neighbours, who had also developed a taste for the cultivated roots but didn't want to stop hunting or see the forests destroyed. They therefore made the occasional minor incursion into Lasse's territory, refusing to recognise his ownership rights and especially his right to destroy the land and the hunt by burn-beating. Lasse had to expel them by armed force. But while the people were at war they couldn't work. Hence the others had to feed and clothe those who were out protecting the fields. And so Lasse levied a general protection tax.

Having given up on the idea of a nomadic lifestyle, people now started building houses. But the pleasure of remaining in one place was dearly bought. From now on Lasse never had a day of rest, and spent all his time settling disputes and drafting new laws and regulations.

Chapter 7

People's customs were becoming increasingly coarse. There had been something invigorating about life on the move in the forests, and people generously gave away the meat they couldn't preserve. Now that they could store things, they became mean and petty. The hunter tribes, who still roved the forests nearby, thought it was shameful to rob the cows of the milk that nature had intended for their calves, and the noble ones among them decided to put a stop to this animal cruelty by force. The hunters had long despised these *calves*, as they called them, and all the more so when they witnessed a slaughter, when the defenceless bound animals were cruelly beaten and bled to death. It was a shocking sight for the hunters, who had seldom seen any death struggle and never any bloodshed. Peter Snagg, who was the hunters' chief, could find no words to express his sorrow and dismay for the growth of this brutality. What was worse, the forests were being burned and people were starting to eat grass 'like animals'. Peter was of the view that the destruction of the forests would spoil the earth. Not only that, he considered it foolish to grow grass seeds when such vast areas of land were taken up by dry straw!

'What filthy, wretched, miserable people!' he exclaimed when he saw them leaning on their hoes and spades. 'They spend all their time poking around in the soil, which only has to be fertilised with droppings again once it's produced its harvest. What kind of people are they? They've become so degenerate they eat dung. At least that's what they slop out of their cowsheds onto the fields, and what they use for growing the crops they haul into their barns. Then they build their huts out of planks, which are packed tightly together and don't allow the air in. And there they sit stinking and stoking up their fires, so that when they come out into the fresh air they feel ill. They see nothing of the outside world apart from their burnt fields and the dung heaps outside their barns. And to think they're skilled people and proud of their occupation!'

Lasse, who still occasionally met with Peter on friendly terms, would always dispute this with him. He maintained that agriculture made the people peaceful as he who kept his harvest under the open sky had to be sure he made no enemies, who might take it away while he slept.

But Peter argued that he who had possessions could never sleep soundly, and would always be worried about losing them. And, he continued, would he still feel attached to the earth, would he find it hard to depart this miserable life when the time came to leave his belongings behind? The driving rain, a hail storm, a falling fence could destroy the fruits of your labours at any time. All this would only produce a fearful tribe. A wretched, slave-like people was all he would be able to make out of these earth-pokers, who would end up firmly convinced that the world consisted solely of their plots of land.

Lasse soon saw the consequences. The bondsmen, who were expensive to feed and difficult to keep watch over, had to be set free. They made straight for the forests and started burn-beating. Soon Lasse's entire province was inhabited by agriculturalists. Disputes arose over plots of forest and pasture grounds. The animals of the one would trample all over the fields of the other. People called for universal agreement, and Lasse was obliged to go off and find the first law of the Statute, or the Code of the Law of the Land, according to which everyone had the right to own the land he had taken for himself. But it soon became clear that the law was not being complied with. So punishments had to be devised. Since there was already a threat of over-population, and prisons were supposed to be an unjust punishment for the innocent and, in fact, everyone wanted to go to prison to be given food and a place to live without having to work, the simplest thing to do would be to kill those who had broken the law. No one was as yet madly passionate about life as, comparing their present life with their former good life back on the Isle of the Blessed, they generally felt that life was a burden.

And so the death penalty was accepted with enthusiasm, and the Criminal Code was reinstated.

There were, however, new complications to consider. Lasse could see that issues were beginning to pile up, but it was impossible to resolve them. He could do no other than to carry on as before.

After several years of heated debate and law-making concerning enclosure obligations, the watercourse, which some people had blocked with mills, thereby making it difficult for others to fish, the rights of way on other people's land, where the only way to access one's own land was to traverse someone else's, and other similar matters, it happened one day that one of the residents, or farmers, as they were now called, who had set up home close to the fields and pasture grounds, suddenly died. He left a wife and six children: three sons and three daughters. They all wanted the farm, but the farm would not be able to feed them all if it were shared between them, and Lasse would rather have one farmer than six crofters. Lasse had to consult the old Code of the Law of Inheritance, which ruled that the son should take over the farm and support the mother. The remaining siblings would have to go out into the world and seek service elsewhere. Alerted to this, the other farmers started to be more careful when it came to having children, and it was seldom the case that a farmer had more than two children, since no one wanted their children to become servants. But those who were already born and had no land to go to started to form a class of disillusioned young people. They were very dangerous; having nothing to lose, they had nothing to fear. They took to the forests, as they could not see why they should go and slave for others who reaped the fruit of their labours. For days on end, Lasse shut himself away with the priest, trying to contrive a reason why some should work while others ate, but they came up with nothing.

However, now that there was no need to parcel out the land into plots, the harvest would occasionally be so great that a surplus was produced, and the farmer would have more foodstuffs than he could eat. So he had the idea of bartering with others who also had surpluses, and they soon knew exactly at what time and in which place they should meet those who had something to trade. People met at the market places, where they would also find hunters with their leather goods, salt, fish and game, which they bartered for seeds, cheese, butter and cattle. To facilitate the barter, they used plates of zinc stamped with numbers, which served as a means of exchange. But when people in this way started to amass wealth, those who were without land or inheritance became so envious they turned to robbery and plundering.

Society was now under grave threat, and Lasse had to enlist an army of regular soldiers from the new disillusioned class, as a result of which the old army increased its numbers, which meant that new taxes had to be levied. The farmers were happy enough to pay the taxes just as long as they were protected. But those good-for-nothings, sitting in their nice new tower, eating, drinking, playing and dancing; they had nothing to do yet considered themselves higher than mere earth-pokers. Their manners were coarse and they had no respect for Lasse. They took to the roads and pathways to rob the traders returning from the market.

For a long time a muffled dissatisfaction could be sensed amongst the farmers, who had no desire to feed tyrants. The death penalty scared no one as they all believed they would return to the Isle of the Blessed after death, and they looked forward to their death as they would a banquet. Lasse was now desperate to find something that would instil in them the fear of death. And he didn't need to look far.

Bah, or the former Pastor Axonius, who had fallen into a kind of bestial apathy, was now awakened and sent out to preach the religion of politics, or hell. The most salient points of this fine doctrine were: all people who do not own land are villains; God has created them but they are disobedient, and disobedience towards superiors is the greatest sin, therefore, all who were without land and did not wish to work for others would go to hell after death, where they would be roasted alive for all eternity. In the beginning this absurd idea failed to make any impression on the people, whose minds were still clear. But great is the power of habituation, and Bah gradually succeeded in making the women fear death through his paintings. This was a step in the right direction. But the soldiers only made fun of the priest, and were quite incorrigible. In the end Lasse had to resort to another method. He bribed them.

The country was divided into states, each of which was governed by one soldier as a chieftain. Now there was some measure of control over the farmers, as each state chieftain had a tower and a garrison. But these chieftains exercised an oppression over the farmers that knew no bounds, and imposed a tax on every trader who travelled through his territory. This tax was called a toll and was supposed to protect the traders (from theft by the so-called 'protectors').

This was how the progressive evolution 'progressed'.

Lasse had married and had children. As his expenses were increasing, he had to raise more income from taxes. But then the farmers complained. They themselves had so many children to feed, they said, that they had no wish to feed anyone else's. And young people were having babies without check. Lasse felt obliged to impose a new law that forbade people who did not own land or property to have children on pain of a hefty fine. To maintain strict control over those who had babies, everyone who wanted to marry was required to notify Bah, who would first instruct them in the doctrine of hell, to which every youth who had reached manhood and every girl old enough to marry were obliged to swear oath. Their parents wailed and complained but to no avail, as henceforth all delicate matters would be decided by the military powers at all stages. There were other considerations too.

The women, who had placed themselves under the protection of the men for their children's sake, had in so doing become dependent upon the men, in much the same way as servants. They did all the minor household chores, and the sisters who were without inheritance looked after the brothers. But since every farmer's boy wanting to marry was worried he would not have the means to do so because of the increased taxes, the girls remained unmarried. Their parents then had the idea of giving them a wedding gift and eventually ceding half of the inheritance right to them. Thus it became easier for those with a large inheritance to marry than it was for those who had very little. As a result, the property owners kept together, unlike those who did not own any land, and this gave rise to a landed nobility, albeit an oppressive and thieving nobility.

But the thieving nobility were anxious lords who still cherished happy memories of their time as hunters. In order to have something with which to appease themselves, they seized possession of the few hunting grounds that remained, and forbade the farmers to bear arms. Another innovation of these thieves, which understandably sparked the farmers' anger, was to tame wolves. But the wolves were only ever tame enough to obey their masters, but not to desist biting everyone else. They were meant to be used for the sake of the hunt, but in fact they were there to protect the stolen goods whilst the thieves slept the sleep of the intoxicated. This companionship between thieves and wild animals infuriated the farmers, but they had lost all hope of having their voices heard.

After a while, the lords started to direct their thirst for hunting against each other, and they would carry out minor forays against each other's towers. The farmers were always the ones who suffered, as their fields were trampled all over by the lords' horses. Without weapons, the farmers were powerless against armed men and wild beasts. They therefore complained to Lasse, who, seeing how things were becoming more and more complicated, could find no other solution than to arm the farmers and, with their help, to use his own soldiers to punish the lords. And so he did.

With this done, it only remained for him to step forward and let himself be proclaimed chief of all chieftains and kings. To add a little glamour to this event, he arranged a grand coronation. Dressed in a red wolfskin fur with a hedgehog skin and a beaver's hat with jay feathers, he asked Bah to smear him around the mouth with tar on an open meadow, and instructed all the people to take a new oath on the doctrine of hell. They were to swear that Lasse had been sent by God, and that the Hulling Dynasty was descended from Japheth, the son of Noah, and hence all the other chieftains were subservient to him and had to pay him tributes. This was not a problem for them, as they simply imposed another tax on their farmers. And so Lasse I of the House of Hulling was anointed and declared King with God's blessing. But to add dignity to the title of King, he had himself named Lasse I Hugo de Hulling von Japhethson.

A period of relative calm ensued. The doctrine of hell had taken hold everywhere, and the fear of death was so great that few crimes were committed.

But a new class of non-landowners had emerged. Some of these, who could no longer roam around freely, since there was now a fine for roaming, had settled close to the state chieftains' towers and made clothes and footwear for the indolent garrison. They received a modest pay, but enjoyed the chieftain's protection. In other words, they had to pay a tax for working for the idlers. But people had become so confused in their minds that the poor tailors and shoemakers could not see this deception. The imposition of the doctrine of hell had made them fear death so much that they would live at any price, under any pressure and in any conditions, rather than risk dying.

But the shoemakers and the tailors also had to eat and drink, and nothing grew around the tower. So the farmers had to bring them food in exchange for clothing, footwear and money. But the chieftains had marked out an area around the tower, where they built a wall. In the wall they installed a gate, and next to the gate a scribe, for they had long been employing scribes to take payment from farmers for the right to enter and sell. The farmers could not understand why they had to pay to go to the trouble of taking food into the town. No one else understood either, but it was 'what was written in the book'.

Eventually, some shrewd merchants approached Lasse and explained that agriculture would fail if the farmers had to keep travelling to town to trade. They took it upon themselves to buy from the farmers, who in return would have to pay a tax to 'The Beaver's Hat', as Lasse was now called. He agreed to the proposal, but the farmers refused to sell. Famine ensued in the town, and the farmers were ordered, on pain of death, to sell to the merchants. Out of spite, the farmers then placed such high prices on their goods that Lasse had to draw up tariffs, which set the prices for the farmers' cattle and grain. So now the town's future was guaranteed, as was the thieves', and peace and happiness reigned for five long months. For this, Lasse's soldiers gave him the name Lasse Byrelock, because it was he who held the key to the farmers' byres, which he opened and closed whenever he pleased.

Chapter 8

The peace was only illusory, however, and nothing that could be relied upon. The old farmers, who had witnessed everything from the beginning, had lost all respect for Lasse. They had once treated him as a brother, but now that he had the power to protect them with military force, they felt exhausted by all the trouble, and gave in. 'What can we do?', they would ask themselves, and as there was nothing they could do, they kept quiet and suffered.

But it was not so easy to subdue the younger generation, who had no wish to obey their father or their mother, and strangers even less. Bah vainly tried to frighten them with hell. They were still young and could think clearly, and they saw that this story was false and made no sense, and they laughed at Bah. They became wild and unruly. They couldn't bear to sit around in unhealthy, foul-smelling huts, but instead would run around the forests and fields, seeking out adventures. Their parents would flog them, but this only induced the boys to set fire to the huts and haystacks and run off into the woods. This time society was under grave threat, and someone seriously suggested that every second boy should be castrated in order to secure a workforce for the future. But Lasse ruled out this unorthodox measure. He had another method, which he had kept in reserve for a long time as he disapproved of it, because it was both unnatural and inhumane. He had been subjected to the treatment himself while still young. It was the most unpleasant experience he had ever had, and the memory of it haunted him still. Every village was to have a penal cell, in which the children would be kept under lock and key for six years. Every day they would become acclimatised to slavery by being half-starved and caned, and by having the doctrine of hell, plus a new moral devised by Lasse and Bah, drummed into them year after year. Thus they would gradually acquire the values and obedience they, not by their nature, owed to their masters. The method was highly unconscionable but had the same effect as castration.

Certainly, time would need to be spent on the writing of instruction books, but there was too much to be lost from not devoting time and thought to the new idea.

When the facility was ready, it was clear to see that its objective had been achieved. The children were locked in early in the morning, and the first thing they learned to do was to keep silent. This was the most important thing of all, for now the upper class, as they were called since 'God' had placed them above the lower class, need not fear any criticism from the lower classes. The second thing was to obey, that is, to act according to the will of others and not to have a will of one's own. The incarceration of many children in one room was a glowing success, as the unwholesome air was damaging to their health, and along with their health, their strength and will also diminished. But the custom of keeping silent, that is, keeping silent about the truth, had an unexpected drawback; the children discovered that saying yes when they were meant to say no had its advantages, such as rewards or exemption from punishments, and hence lies became abundant. For its part, obedience gave rise to falseness. The children thought it was wrong to hold a friend down while the teacher thrashed him, but they were acting contrary to what they thought was right, and they gradually got used to acting against their own conviction. Those who were the best at lying and told the most falsehoods were praised and given gingerbread and honey cakes, while those who told the truth and were honest were flogged and went without food. Thus the foundation was laid for education. Lasse was sometimes surprised at the results, but what was he to do now that he had driven himself into a corner?

However, it was difficult for the child beaters to fill the long teaching hours with thrashing alone, and new subjects for teaching had to be found. In addition to lies and falsity, a whole host of other untruths were now being taught at school. These were inculcated into the pale and sickly children under the generic title of 'morals'. The first moral was: God hath created farmers and manual workers, and they should work for those who do not want to work. The second moral: Thou shalt be content with thy lot! (For those who had the enviable lot of not having to work, it was not hard to execute this command, but for those whose fate it was to labour and toil, it was quite impossible.) The third moral: Thou shalt not mate if thou hast not twelve acres of land or Bah's permission. (An older boy who objected that the moral should have been: 'Thou shalt have helped thyself to twelve acres of land to be able to mate!' was thrown into a dark cellar.) The fourth moral: Thou must not take other people's belongings. (A girl who said she could remember when her father took his belongings from public property and that her father should therefore be punished was persuaded with the help of a dozen lashes that she was wrong.) The fifth moral: Thou shalt not kill anyone! (A young child who asked whether *thou* also meant Lasse and the executioner, who killed anyone that didn't want to kill the huntsmen in the woods, was placed in stocks.) The sixth moral: Thou must not even think that what we have now can be bad. (This was the finest of all morals as it kills all thought and hence nips all opposition in the bud!)

This did not help, however. The young people feigned and lied, but sometimes the truth would show through and society would be threatened again. People were so tired of living they would allow their work and everything they had to go to wrack and ruin. They themselves starved, but then the upper class would also begin to starve and feel ill, and that would not do. There was no longer any fear of hell as people saw that they already had a hell on earth, and that there could not be anything worse. Lasse and Bah soon found themselves forced to make several timely revisions to the doctrine of hell, and now the priests started to speak more about the happiness in heaven that awaited all those who had suffered and had a hard life. The assertion voiced by some people in opposition, that Lasse and the upper class, who had lived well, would have to go to hell as a consequence, had no effect on the matter, as those in opposition were burnt at the stake and their questions remained unanswered. But discipline was weakened by the prospect of going to heaven, and new methods had to be sought. Lasse now hoaxed several good-for-nothings who didn't want to work into composing verse for the edification of the lower class. And so a band of poets was established. They were poorly dressed, although they had no need to be as they received a wage from the state. But their appearance was meant to make the lower class believe they had evolved from the 'rank and file'. They went around chanting about how marvellous life was; that the good should be seen in all people; that all Lasses, Bahs, local chieftains, parents, guardians and educators were so nice and wished the lower class well; that all discontent with the fact that some worked whilst others ate was just envy and malice; that if each individual tended to his own affairs then everything would be fine, come what may; that tilling the soil and manual labour was not simply toil but the true work, the most arduous work that God had assigned to the leaders, the military powers and the Bahs; that the world *must* be accepted for what it was (even what it had become through the misdemeanours of the Lasses and the Bahs). All this had a great effect. First the verse was learned by heart, then it remained in the ears before penetrating into the mind.

But soon the lower class also started using verse to rail against the upper class. Lasse viewed the approaching storm with horror, but it was not for nothing that he had been learning from the past. At first he tried giving the singers of the verse a salary from the state. That helped for a while, but he became inundated with singers who wanted a wage, and so he raised the taxes. Then, when nothing else worked, he found himself compelled to establish a coterie. Seventeen of the worst singers were selected and proclaimed to be infallible. All the others who wanted to sing the songs were declared incompetent. This helped matters. At the schools, the people who paid the seventeen only to be scolded by them soon became accustomed to regarding the seventeen as infallible and all the others as incompetent. And so all the dissatisfied singers were silenced as, naturally, none of them wanted to go there without at least receiving some praise from the seventeen, which meant that from now on all songs would be sung to the same tune.

The schools increased in number, and it was very difficult to provide everyone with the books of morals. Lasse was obliged after long deliberation, since he was wary of allowing such a dangerous invention to become universally available, to set up a printing press. But to ensure that the potentially harmful device would not be used against him and his works, he had it placed under royal surveillance. The first piece of work produced by the royal printing press was a Decree on the Freedom of the Press. One evening, when the new decree had just been issued, the secret society of The Malcontents arranged a meeting in a hayloft. Paul the Hunter had obtained a copy and wanted to subject it to scrutiny. Everyone took their places to listen to him read it out.

Paul started to read: 'Decree on the Freedom of the Press. Section 1. Every citizen has complete freedom to state their view in print!'

'Hurrah for freedom!' replied The Malcontents.

'Section 2.' Paul read. 'Being of God, the true evangelical doctrine of hell shall not be subjected to undue criticism.'

'What!' cried The Malcontents. 'That's exactly what should be criticised above all else.'

'Section 3.' Paul read. 'Every author has a duty to write in praise of Lasses, Bahs, chieftains, soldiers, writers and child beaters, as well as their friends and acquaintances.'

'Section 4. The Society for Reciprocal Praise, or the 17 Infallibles[3], shall suppress any attempt to produce writings opposing the morals.'

---

[3] This is most probably a satire on the 18 'Immortals' - members of the Swedish Academy.

He was interrupted by Rudolph the Miner. 'Let's remind ourselves what is meant by the morals!'

Paul the Hunter reminded them. 'The morals are: 1) that all farmers and manual workers are born to work for Lasse, Bah, etc.; 2) no one without at least twelve acres of land or Bah's permission may mate.'

'Enough, enough!' exclaimed The Malcontents. 'We remember only too well. Just get on with it!'

'Section 5. No one apart from the Society for Reciprocal Praise may state their view on a deceased Lasse.

'Section 6. Every citizen has complete freedom to state their view in print!'

The Malcontents departed, having firmly resolved to make use of the new freedom of the press at the earliest opportunity.

The child beaters were the first to receive the works of the freedom of the press. The *Book of Morals* was printed in thousands, pinned up in huts and disseminated amongst the lower class, as the upper class, who had written the book, could already recite it by heart.

Lasse was becoming old and weary, and he felt that his days were numbered. He assembled two thousand soldiers and let them elect a successor to the throne. The choice fell to his son, who was immediately hailed as Lasse II Axel[4]. Lasse was moved to tears at such a magnanimous demonstration of the people's affection for his house, and he used the occasion to propose that the beaver's hat and the chair would be hereditary within his family. As the chieftains were clearly displeased, Bah came forward and

---

[4] A tongue-in-cheek reference to the peculiarly Swedish nomenclature of the monarchy, e.g. Gustav II Adolf.

appealed to the people, who were standing a long way off in the woods behind the soldiers. The people, who hated the soldiers and had not heard them say anything other than no, naturally said yes, and now the soldiers had to concede. Lasse expressed his thanks for this renewed show of the people's love, and he saw this as a cry from 'the rank and file' as if God himself had spoken. For the voice of the People is the voice of God, and Lasse II lost no time in adopting the motto, as eloquent as it was untrue, 'the love of the people is my reward!'[5]

Trembling from such diversity of emotions, Lasse lay down on his death bed, exhausted by age and honour. After forgiving his enemies for all their crimes and accepting Bah's assurance of heaven, he fell asleep. All of the 17 Infallibles wrote songs in praise of his eventful life, and Bah held a funeral oration with the words, 'Blessed are the dead, those who die in the Lord.' Lasse II dried his tears and ascended the throne.

---

[5] The motto of King Karl XIV Johan (Bernadotte)

Chapter 9

Lasse II Axel was a fair ruler, who abhorred war but appreciated civilisation and science. His first task as monarch was to write Lasse I's history. The 17 Infallibles were given the assignment, and succeeded in producing a masterpiece of lasting value. In it Lasse was called the Great, and with good reason, as he had founded the new Social Order and had always made the welfare of the people his top priority. But the society of The Malcontents wrote a more candid history of Lasse, in which they bluntly referred to him as 'Hulling the Stupid'. They explained that it was he who had introduced the existing regime of slavery, which deprived as well as provided, and had taxes for the workers and tax exemptions for the idlers. That he had destroyed the young by establishing prisons and child beaters, that he was an imbecile and his society was foolish. The book was confiscated and burned, along with its authors. The Society for Reciprocal Praise now offered a reward of six pounds of zinc to the person who could compose the most eloquent memorial to Lasse I Hugo the Great.

As Lasse II Axel understood that society's discontent could not be stifled overnight, he issued instructions for a history of the kingdom to be written. This relied on the copies of Rudbeck's *Atlantica*, bequeathed by Lasse, his father, to prove incontrovertibly that the present kingdom was in fact the most perfect of all kingdoms, and that this was *Atlantica* itself, or the Isle of the Blessed. The island their forefathers had inhabited, where they had imagined they were living in bliss, had never existed. It was just a fabrication of The Malcontents, to make people unhappy.

The child beaters now introduced a new school book, which was called *The Eminence of the Present* or *The Most Perfect of Societies*.

However, a great many writer children and soldier children had grown up. In order to avoid dissent and division in elections for the king, occupations were made hereditary. But because there was no obstacle to writers and soldiers mating without having twelve acres of land, since they were naturally placed above the laws they had created, the land was soon swarming with upper class children who had no occupation. They were maintained by the state on subsidies or salaries, so that they would have no need to steal or murder, and occupations were found for as many people as possible. But as those without an occupation found it difficult to do nothing, they thought up all manner of trifling professions, all to some degree idiotic. One person would collect buttons, a second would collect cones from fir, pine and juniper trees. A third secured a grant to travel and see the world. This person had returned home after discovering an obsolete language, which had been carved on wooden tablets, and was easy to decipher. The discoverer called the language the Scho-scho dialect, and felt proud of knowing a language no one else did. The button collector had amassed a formidable collection. As he needed somewhere to keep them, he was granted from the state coffers the funds to build a house in which to store his collection. Here he applied himself to the task of putting the buttons in order. They could be divided up into many different categories: underwear buttons, trouser buttons, coat buttons, etc. But our man devised a more artificial and hence more complex system. For this, however, he needed help. Firstly, he wrote a treatise on *The Necessity of the Study of Buttons from a Scientific Point of View*. He then submitted to the Treasury an application for the position of Professor of Buttonology, together with two assistants. The application was approved, but more for the sake of giving those without any occupation something to do than for its own merits, which as yet could not be evaluated. The assistant positions did not need to be advertised, as the man, who was called Hylling (people thought he was born to the Hulling family without Bah's permission), happened to have two sons but could not afford to pay the child beaters to assist in raising them. Hylling would soon amaze the world with the first complete scientific system. He had spent two years developing it, and it was an impressive piece of work as all the buttons in the world could be categorised into its classes.

The system looked as follows:

BUTTONS

Zinc   Copper Tin Iron   Bone   Wood
With holes:------------------------------------
Class   1: With 1 hole   etc.
  "   2   "   2 holes
  "   3   "   3   "
  "   4   "   4   "

Without holes:
Class   1: Without 1 hole   etc.
  "   2   "   2 holes
  "   3   "   3   "
  "   4   "   4   "

With eyes:
   a) *round eyes*   etc.
      A) grooved
      B) grooveless

   b) *oval eyes*
      A) grooved
         1) short-grooved
         2) long-grooved
      B) grooveless
         1) vacant
         2) vacant

It created an unprecedented sensation.

But the man who had been collecting cones did not want to be out-done, and he soon delighted the world with a major artificial system of classifying all cones into 67 classes, 23 families and 1,500 species.

It had long been the intention to expand the range of educational courses and, since it had been considered unfair that the lower class children should learn just as much as those from the upper class, it was decided to establish a university. They already had three sciences: the Scho-scho Dialect, Buttonology and Conology, and henceforth these would be made compulsory subjects. But as the monied farmers and manual workers sent their children to university too, colloquia, or private discussion groups, were set up. Only upper class children could be admitted to these, and without them, examinations could not be taken. However, if a child from the lower class did manage to pass the exam one way or another, he would still not be given an occupation, as occupations were hereditary.

Lasse II Axel died, which could not be prevented, but he earned the posthumous title of Lasse The Wise.

Chapter 10

The son who now acceded the throne called himself quite simply Anders VII. Although the reasons for this are not known, it is believed there is a historical explanation. Under his rule the fine arts developed. As an example, a baker's boy once stood kneading some dough, out of which he was meant to make a horse, but he made a goat instead. The professor of the Scho-scho language happened to be passing by the window where the boy was working, and was amazed at his great talents. He asked him to make a goat from clay instead of dough, which he later fired in the oven.

The invention of the art of painting was a different matter. It had long been observed that in a particular isolated area of the island a number of unemployed collier boys were taking coal and drawing with it on the mine-heads. At first they drew obscenities but then they would draw everything they saw. They drew tables, chair legs, houses, trees, stones, carrots, wheelbarrows, dogs, cats, anything they could get hold of. Their parents tried in vain to get them to drop their fads and fancies and do something useful, but it was impossible. They protested and said they would rather starve and die than stop drawing. It was a veritable mania.

When the matter came to the attention of Anders, he felt very sorry at first, as he loved his people as only a prince could. He then had them confined to a house, where they could devote themselves to their mania unhindered and under royal protection. He conducted experiments with them, and one day he had fifty maniacs draw one and the same chair leg. But it was found that no two drawings were alike. Philosophers were summoned, and they explained that it depended on individual interpretation. Anders, who had not believed that the individual interpretation of a chair leg could be anything philosophical, now realised his mistake and believed that the profound meaning of the drawing was a moment in the life of the spirit, and he had the most skilful artist declared a professor. The latter lost no time in writing a thesis on the form and content of the drawing. From the well-chosen example of a chair leg, which was the prize subject, he deduced: the chair leg's content was the individual interpretation, the chair leg's form was the drawing. When content and form eclipsed one another, or became completely fused with each other, then the drawing was a perfect drawing, or one of beauty. Everything that was drawn was beautiful; a defaecating cow was not beautiful because nature was not beautiful, but a defaecating cow that was drawn was beautiful because it was diffused with the individual interpretation of a defaecating cow.

One day they found a rather unflattering drawing of Anders VII on the external façade of the drawing house. People walking past started to laugh. The artist was summoned and instructed to draw the king but in a good way. The artist stated that his drawing was good as it was diffused with and defined by his individual interpretation of Anders VII. The artist was ordered, on pain of death, to change his individual interpretation of Anders VII immediately. Since the artist was promised the title and salary of a professor, he did change his individual interpretation of Anders VII immediately, whereupon he was appointed court artist.

Anders passed away in the eighth year of his rule, and was called by the 17 Infallibles the Patron of the Arts. He was succeeded in line by Per Erik I. He was a fierce ruler who could not stay in one place. He waged war with the hunters and would himself slay as many people as he could. But the people complained of the war taxes and couldn't see the point of all these slayings. To enlighten them, Per had a new school book compiled, which was to be introduced in schools. It was called *The Book of Kings* and contained texts extolling all the kings from Lasse I to Per Erik; in particular it praised all incursions into and plundering of foreign kingdoms.

Warfare continued under Per Erik, however, as the military men loved honour and especially the conquest of other people's property, such as ornamental clocks, china sets and coins. This gave a member of the society of The Malcontents cause to write a pamphlet entitled *A Comparison of the Various Types of Stealing, Private and Public,* or *Theft from the Perspective of State Law,* together with a *Table Showing International Thefts under the Most Recent Kings of the House of Hulling.* As usual, the pamphlet was burnt along with the author. Per Erik died as a result of inebriation, and (as writers of history, we are obliged to stick to the painful truth) perhaps also of some fornication. He was mourned by all men of war and was called The Hero King or The Irreconcilable.

The Hulling Family, which had begun with The Great Lasses, died out with him. As it had already been drummed into the emerging generation that the kings were of God, it now felt odd to elect a king from among the natives, since the people would not be able to comprehend that someone who was a soldier chieftain yesterday could be elected by the people today to be of God. An expedition was therefore despatched to the distant tribes. The expedition members duly returned with a subject, who was hastily baptised and crowned. So that he would be loved, he was given the name Lasse III and was said to have belonged to the Hulling Family generations back. As he neither spoke the language nor knew anything about the country he was to govern, the power chanced to fall into the hands of Bah (a descendant of Pastor Axonius from Uppsala). He did everything to inculcate the doctrine of hell, and instructed the professors in the artists' house to create a drawing of hell, which was to be hung up in all the churches. Lasse died and was given the posthumous title of Saint Lasse.

Under his successor, Per II Erik, a terrible war of religion broke out between the provinces. An idealist had come forward and declared that the unfortunates in hell were not in fact pinched with tongs, but stabbed with forks. A major ecumenical council was convened, and for sixteen days and sixteen nights the issue was debated between the parties, who were given the names Tongs and Forks[6]. The question was resolved in the Tongs' favour. But the Forks stood their ground, and didn't even yield at the threat of being burnt at the stake. They had to defend themselves against the onslaught of the Tongs. But the Forks were the superior power in one province, and the Tongs now found themselves cornered and sent for help from Per II Erik. Per Erik summoned his people together and, with tears in his eyes, swore he would defend the true doctrine of hell even if his life depended on it. And so he

---

[6] Most probably a satire on the political feud between the Caps and the Hats in the Swedish *Riksdag* (Parliament) in the 18th century.

went to war. This lasted fifteen years. Grandfather clock chests were sent home one after the other, and there was an endless conscription of people and levying of taxes. But the Forks defended themselves with valour. Eventually the dreadful news came that Per Erik had fallen. But their grief was eased to some extent when they learned that the Tongs had taken two provinces, six thousand flags and drums, five hundred grandfather clocks and three million in gold and silver. Per Erik's body was brought home and a church was erected over his remains with the following inscription: *To the Hero King, the True Defender of the Doctrine of Hell, Died for his Tong. His Spirit lies truly with God!*

This was the most eloquent page in the Hullings' book of fame. But the Forks continued to stand by their faith and in the end were allowed to practise their religion freely. Nevertheless, there were still people (from amongst The Malcontents) who claimed that what they were fighting over was nonsense, because it made no difference whether you were poked with forks or tongs in hell when you knew there was no hell.

Per Erik's successor was Jöns I Philip, who introduced plays to keep The Malcontents in high spirits. But when The Malcontents also performed drama, their plays were declared sinful, and a national playhouse was established, in which plays from the *Book of Fame* and the *War of the Tongs against the Infidels* were performed. Through this the people learned to show respect for their 'great history'.

Under his successor, Jöns II Petter, the *State News* newspaper was established. This was prompted in part by the discontent that had been fermenting and in part by the need to spread the opinion of the upper class as rapidly as possible. The objectives of the *State News* were: to constantly explain that everything the lower class thought, said and wrote was lies; that all actions of the lower class were dictated by base urges, self-advantage, envy and ill-will; to explain that the present society was the most perfect society, and was paving the way to bliss for everyone; to preach that the doctrine of hell was the mildest, most profound and wisest of all teachings, and that it should never be replaced by any other; that all other teachings were stupid and immoral, etc. This invention was greeted with jubilation and the *State News* thereafter took the title of *Universal Opinion* or *Blessed Stagnation.*

Chapter 11

Society had now reached its apogee or ideal of preposterousness. What was useful was held in contempt while the useless was honoured. Thus it was more honourable to draw an apple, for which you could be made professor and knighted, than to grow an apple tree, on which you would only become liable to pay tax. Performing in a play was respected and honoured far more highly than writing a play, and at times you could see the public crowding around an actress's carriage to whisk her away from the theatre after watching an exceptionally good performance. Everyone who wanted to obstruct justice, hinder improvement of the miserable situation, increase destitution and punish the innocent, were rewarded by titles, pensions and badges of honour.

Most ideal of all was the development of life in the towns. In the royal city, three hundred thousand people lived in an area that was no bigger than a few acres. And when you looked at this stone grave, which was the town's pride, it was possible to calculate at a glance how many loads of dirt it stood on, for it was not every day that the town was cleaned.

This produced a stench which, although not noticed by the town's inhabitants, caused diseases. The idealistic way in which the city was built also contributed to this to a great extent; instead of being placed in rows that faced the sun, the houses had been built in long strips with paths running between them so narrow that only a small number of inhabitants ever had any light in their rooms. Just as some people who live in valleys between high mountains can contract certain illnesses, here too there were those who suffered from a condition called degeneracy, which alters the brain's functions and makes idiocy hereditary.

The town dwellers too became so degenerate that the farmers could not understand what they were saying. Their thoughts and ideas had become so confused in their minds that those who could afford it would sleep during the day and eat and drink at night, which naturally gave rise to even more diseases.

Cramped together into a tiny area, where they were forced to disturb each other, shove each other and trample on each other, they were constantly at each other's throats. Symptomatic of the rise in degeneracy was a helplessness resembling that of a child. As a result, many thousand gold marks had to be paid to the watchmen, who, under the title of police, wandered around the streets, took home those who were drunk, carried home those who had got run over, ran to fetch water for those who had fainted, located house numbers, explained where the barber lived, where call girls could be found, where fire had broken out, and so on and so forth.

All the girls and boys who did not have any landed property to inherit flocked from the countryside to this idiot dwelling. The boys were taken on as slaves, the girls sought placements as slaves or waited for an opportunity to be defiled. For it was difficult for young men in the town to get married, and hence all the girls were defiled with the police's and their own consent, and their children would then have no claim to any occupation or office.

Unhappy as they were in the towns, they sought lasting remedies in alcoholic beverages, which were consumed in public places. Whenever alcohol was drunk in large quantities, which only ever happened in male company, a special kind of alcohol would be drunk for the woman at home, who could not leave her children, plus a glass for the home, where a bed and a housewife were waiting. When they became very inebriated, they would drink a large glass of alcohol for the king and one for the fatherland, sometimes also for the pure doctrine of hell.

The whole of this ideal society of three hundred thousand inhabitants claimed to be working for the good of the people. But they only needed to go down to the customs house and the market in the mornings to see who was really feeding them. In remuneration for the food they supplied to the town, the farmers received a small amount of money, which went on taxes. They could then look at oil paintings and listen to recitals and plays, which they had no time for, although that was their own fault as they were at liberty to listen to them whenever they liked, for a small charge of course. They would also get teachers, who taught them the doctrine of hell and the *Book of Fame*, for a small charge of course, as well as an ear-full of lecturing from the priest on Sundays, who reminded them they were nothing but swindlers who ought to be castrated if they did not pay their taxes. All of these so-called 'blessed fruits of education' the farmers received (for a small charge) in exchange for bringing food to those who would have starved to death if they failed one morning to come to market. Such was the extent to which the farmers had been duped!

But the town's poor and discontent were ever present, and in the end these would have to be dealt with as they were becoming dangerous. For their sakes, public hospices were set up. These were called prisons, where experiments were carried out to see how little a person could live on.

And when this was ascertained, the workers were found to be over-indulging. When the workers refused to work because work was not compulsory, work was made compulsory, and they were compelled to work by arms.

The discontent and ferment eventually became too great and the taxes became intolerable. The blame for all this was dumped on the regent. In the end, he invented a new system of government, which, after much ado, was accepted under the title of the parliamentary system, or the system of accountability. Just as the Decree on the Freedom of the Press required a great many newspaper editors to circumvent this blame by placing so-called accountability assessors in their own position, the king now appointed ministers who were held accountable for his stupidities, thereby protecting the king against all prosecution. But the extent of the risk that this accountability posed was only that one minister, who had been a scapegoat for one of the king's follies, had to vacate his post as rural chieftain and knight cherubim. Hence these accountability assessor positions were also very agreeable and sought-after.

Closely linked to this was the gossipmonger system, or the parliamentary system of governance. A group of rich people would assemble once a year and through clever speeches sought to select the next victim on whom to impose a new tax. When they became too clever for each other, they would either come to an amicable agreement not to levy taxes on each other, or haggle over the tax burdens.

A particularly good example of this system of governance was the parliamentary act that governed the tannery industry. For twenty-five years six tanners had been producing poor leather at poor prices. Then one day the hunters, who still lived nearby, started to import good leather at good prices. The people rejoiced at the news, but the six tanners, who had seats in the parliamentary chamber, put forward a demand that tax should be paid on the hunters' leather. Local industry had to be protected, the country's children could not be devoured, etc. And so they received tax on the hunters' leather! For the sake of these six tanners, the people had to continue to buy poor leather at poor prices. This system was called the protection system, since it enabled private interest to be protected at public expense. The accountability assessor, however, felt he should apply for the position of country chieftain, feigned indignation and left. He then attained his position along with the Order of the Cherubims, which was only awarded to men of standing.

But the saddest thing of all was that degeneracy gradually became hereditary, like physical weaknesses. The degenerates, who were called the Intelligence Set (from Latin *intelligere,* to understand) because they could not see their degeneracy (or *lucus* from *non lucere*), had degenerated so much that they were no longer conscious of the softening of their brains and, on the contrary, considered themselves the wisest people in society. Since they had the military powers at their command, society very soon assumed the semblance of a mental asylum, in which the inmates had revolted and locked up the wardens and doctors. This gave rise to the most absurd behaviour. Hence it was possible to hear opinions being defended in all earnestness in the parliamentary chamber. For example, that Atlantica, as the kingdom was now called, possessing 50,000 fighting forces, would be able to defend itself against Aquilonia, or any other kingdom, which had twenty times as many forces. On another occasion, someone had successfully asserted the opinion that society would break down altogether if the people did not want to pay tax to certain comedians. And on still another, that the state would collapse if the people refused to grant a salary and professorship to a gentleman who had displayed a large number of beetles on zinc pins.

As a gradual consequence of seeing degeneracy valued, rewarded and sought after year in and year out, many of the unfortunates wanted to be a part of the degeneracy, because it brought honour and money. Now it was to be spread throughout the schools, but this did not happen quickly, as people's minds still clung to the memory of the old ways, which had made a lot of sense, even if they were worse in many respects. But constantly seeing that the only thing that afforded them respect was to share the opinions of the powerful, they were forced, against their will, at least to express the accepted opinions even if they were not their own. And when they had finally succeeded in adopting the same views as those held by the people above them, these views were already out-dated.

Thus there developed an interminable hunt, an eternal friction and unrest in society, and a discontent that never saw any let-up. And when the powerless rose up *en masse* against the powerful and divested them of their power, it could be seen straightaway how history repeated and renewed itself. Thus, after every act of uprising, those who had recently been the oppressed would become the oppressor, which they had always dreamed of.

Then it was as though the entire thinking population would throw themselves into a frenzy in an effort to put a stop to all the troubles, poverty and quarrels at whatever cost, and there arose a number of sects, fired by a holy zeal to improve society.

One sect, called the Moleskin Academy, defended the opinion that society should grow in peace just like a natural meadow, where grass and weeds had to fight for whatever food there was, even at risk of the stronger weeds dominating.

Another one, called the Socialists or The Little Birds School, strove for a unified community of the inferior, the sick, the weak, the stupid, the lazy, whereby the right of the weaker to oppress the stronger should he held sacred in constitutional law.

A third sect, named the Boschman Sect, believed that the only salvation lay not in a solution to matters that were insolvable, but in blowing up the entire planet of Tellus, which, having been created from nothing, it would be safer to return to its original state.

And whilst these and other sects fought for supremacy, society continued to become the society of old, searching for evidence in the past of how the present excelled in all aspects, assuming the forms it had previously assumed, dictating resolutions and enacting laws, so that never before had there reigned so much harmony amongst the rulers, who believed and considered it proven that this was the true Isle of the Blessed, while the ruled were constantly strengthened in their old belief that it was most definitely of the unblessed.

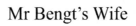

Mr Bengt's Wife

'Love? Why, desire, of course!' the young count replied to his elderly mentor as the two of them sat conversing in the ship's cabin below deck, to pass the time whilst waiting for sufficient wind to start them on their journey from Älvsnabben to the University of Prague.

'No, young Sir!' replied school master Franciskus Olai. 'There's more to it than that. It's something quite different, something neither lofty theology nor profound philosophy has yet been able to define. In this age of excessive wisdom people have too little faith, but from this it follows that they had too much faith before. I was around to witness the beginning of this age, when I helped to demolish the venerated old structures; the ancient and dilapidated temple of arrogance and self-interest. I tore up the pages of the holy books and tore down the pictures from the church walls. I contributed to the closing of the monasteries, and followed the old faith. But, my dear Sir, there are things that the Lord Almighty has created himself, and we'd do well to leave these things alone. Now let's turn our attention to Amor, or love; the fire that burns brightly when it burns the right way, but which can quickly go out if it burns the wrong way, and can even turn into hatred if it goes really wrong.'

'When does it burn the right way, then? That can't be very often!' said the count, making himself more comfortable on his bunk.

'As often as not, love appears like a flash of lightning from the heavens when it comes, and it's stronger than our will and our reason combined. But people are different, and whether it lives on or not depends upon the person. For people are born with different natures and dispositions, like birds or other creatures. Some are like the wood fowl, the capercaillie and the black grouse, where the male has an entire seraglio, like the Great Turk. Why this is so, we don't know, but that's how it is, it's their nature. Others are like little birds that take a partner for each year and then find another. And still others, such as the dove, are truly affectionate and build a life together, and when one partner dies the other loses the desire to live.'

'Have you seen any doves yourself, amongst humankind?' asked the count, dubiously.

'I have seen a great many, my dear Sir. I have seen black grouse that have taken doves, and the dove was very unhappy. I have seen dove cocks that have had cuckoos. And the cuckoo is the worst of all birds, as it only indulges in the lust and neglects to raise its young, and throws it out of the nest. But I have also seen doves.'

'That were never pecked?'

'On the contrary, they were pecked when the cage was cramped and food was in short supply. But they were good friends all the same; that's love, you see. There is also a sea bird, or gull, which is called a velvet scoter. Gulls always stay together as a pair. If you shoot the one, the other doesn't fly away but comes closer and allows itself to be shot, and that's why the velvet scoter is the most foolish bird of all.'

'That's because it's on heat, master!'

'No, young Sir, they stay together for life. And the springtime is their time of passion. In the winter, when they're left alone without their young, they never part from each other, but eat together, hunt together, sleep together. That's not heat, that's love, and if the tender emotion is present in a simple creature, why should it not be present in a human being?'

'I've heard that it *is* present in humans, but it is apt to disappear after the wedding.'

'It's lust that disappears, to some extent, but that's when love makes its appearance.'

'That's just friendship - if it exists.'

'Quite right, my dear Sir. But friendship between people of different sexes - that's just what love is. But there's so much to it, there are so many aspects, and so many facets to those aspects. If you're willing, I could tell you a story about something I have seen for myself, and from which you might learn a thing or two. It happened in my youth, some forty years ago, but I remember every little detail as if it happened yesterday. May I relate it to you?'

'Go ahead, master! Time passes slowly when you're lying in wait for a head wind. But bring some candles and some wine before you start, as I believe your story is not going to keep us awake.'

'You, Sir, probably. It has kept *me* awake far too many nights,' replied Franciskus, and left to fetch the items requested.

When he returned and they had both made themselves comfortable on their bunks, he began.

'This is the story of Mr Bengt's wife:

'She was born of noble parentage at the beginning of this century. She had a strict upbringing, and on the death of her parents she was placed in a convent by her guardian. There she was distinguished by her exalted religious zeal; she practised self-flagellation on Fridays and fasted every major feast day. When she reached the age of puberty, her condition became more precarious, and she even made attempts to take her own life by starving herself, as she considered it consistent with a Christian's duties to mortify the flesh and live close to God. There then occur two events that are turning points in her life. Her guardian flees the country after squandering her fortune. The convent then changes its attitude towards her, as the convent was a secular institution that kept its doors closed to the afflicted and the poor. When she sees this, she becomes beset by doubt. Doubt was the sickness of the age, and she became sorely infected. Her companions believed in nothing, and her superiors didn't believe in much either. One day she was sent away on an errand for the sick. On the way - a beautiful, lonely road through the forest - she met a horseman; young, strong and handsome. She stopped and looked at him, as if beholding a revelation. He was the first man she had seen for five years and, indeed, the first she had seen since becoming a woman. He held his horse back a moment, greeted her - and rode on. From that day she grew weary of the convent, and life enticed her. Life in all its beauty and ardour drove her away from Christ, and she suffered tribulations and outbursts, so that she now spent most of her time in the penal chamber. One day she received a letter that had been smuggled in to her via the caretaker. It was from the horseman. He lived on the other side of the lake, and she could see his castle from the window of the penal chamber. There was a continuous exchange of letters. Vague rumours were circulating that the church was about to undergo a major reform, that the monasteries too were to be abolished and their inhabitants absolved from their oath.

'This aroused hope within her. But as she now discovered that it was possible to be absolved from an oath, she lost faith in the sanctity of the oath, and suddenly all bonds were broken. From now on she only believed in the eternal right of her instincts in the face of the laws of society and the church.

'In the end she was betrayed by a false friend, and the discovery of the exchange of letters resulted in the imposition of physical punishment. But destiny had decreed otherwise, and on the very day when the punishment was to be administered, a message arrived from the king and the estate of the realm with an order to close the convent. The messenger is no other than her own knight in armour. And he opens up the convent's gates to her, to offer her her freedom and his hand.

'There ends the first part of her life journey.'

'First part?' The count reached for the pitcher of wine. 'They found each other. Isn't that where the story ends?'

'No, Sir, that's where it ends in the sagas, but in reality it is precisely where it begins. I recall the day after the wedding; I was their priest and had wed them. The breakfast table had been set, and they emerged from the bridal chamber radiant, as if the whole earth was dancing for their sake and the sun had been placed in the sky to shine upon them alone. He was full of vitality, and felt capable of bearing the entire world on his shoulders, and all his thoughts were devoted to making their life as good and happy as ever he could. She was so ecstatic she could neither eat nor drink, and all she wanted to do was forget that the sinful world existed. She still had her fancies from former times, when heaven meant everything and the earth nothing; he was the son of the new age, who knew that a life on earth was necessary for admission to heaven afterwards.'

'And then things started to go downhill?' interrupted the count.

'They went downhill, as you say. I remember how he ate his breakfast with voracity, while she just sat and looked at him. When she spoke of the singing of the birds, he would talk about roast veal! He once noticed that she had thrown her clothes on a chair in the dining room the evening before, and he reminded her that order had to be observed in a house.'

'And, of course, it all fell apart at the seams.'

'It wasn't as bad as that. But it did draw a cloud in front of her sun, and she felt that it opened up clefts between them. But she closed her eyes to them, as she would have done had she been walking in the mountains. Then it clouded over a second time. His thoughts were heavy, secretive. He wanted to leave her for a while to go and work in the fields as his crops had been stooked, and he knew that his livelihood depended on them. But she asked him to stay and not talk about the soil that day!'

'The soil? What a dolt!'

'Yes, quite! That's how she had been raised. It was the convent's fault that she had learnt to show contempt for God's creation. So he stayed at home and proposed a hunt, and she agreed with great pleasure.'

'A hunt! Well, there's a fine thing!'

'Yes, Sir, so they thought at the time - every age has its whims. But then the clouds come once again, and it wasn't the luckiest of days for the young horseman. The king's bailiff had paid him a visit and asked to speak with the knight alone. The conversation was granted, and the knight was informed that, according to the new law, he stood to lose his noble status if he didn't pay what had been owing for his armour for the past five years. He couldn't pay straightaway, but the bailiff promised him a payment extension of one year if he offered up the farm as a security. The necessary arrangements were made. But then the question arose whether he should inform his wife of the matter. He summoned me to ask me my advice. I thought it was a pity the young woman's dreams of happiness and bliss should be dashed so soon, and I committed the indiscretion of advising that she should not be informed of the situation regarding the house before the year was out.'

'You were right to do so! For why should women get involved in these matters? It would have just brought grief and trouble and the poor man would never have got any peace.'

'No, young Sir, I was wrong to do so. Because in a proper marriage a husband and wife should have complete trust in each other and act in unison, even when they're not in bed.

'And what was the consequence of this? Throughout that year they grew apart. She lived in her rose garden, and he on the fields. He kept secrets from her and worked desperately without seeking her advice. They each lived their own separate life. When they happened to meet, he would feign cheerfulness, and so their entire life became false. In the end, he became tired and withdrew into himself. And so did she.'

'And their love came to an end?'

'No, Sir. That might have been possible, but true love endures worse disasters than this. They still loved each other, and this would become apparent after the trials they were about to undergo.

'She had her child, and her life journey took an entirely new direction. She had less need of her husband as her time was now taken up by her caring for the child. Her husband felt at greater liberty, as there was less of a demand on his affection than before. She threw herself with her heart and soul into the new tasks that were thrust upon her. She remained alert at night and was sluggish during the day, and she would never entrust her child to a wet nurse. Reality and life, with all their intricacies, at first appeared to intoxicate her empty soul, and she even started to find pleasure in talking with her husband about his fields and ploughing. But this couldn't last long. Our upbringing remains within us like the seeds of a weed, which can lie dormant in the soil a year or two, but after proper cultivation, the weed shoots up again, and it's never a good idea to replant old trees. One day she looked in the mirror and found that she had grown pale, gaunt and unattractive. She saw that she had passed her prime and that her beauty was not what it once was. Then awoke the woman within her, that part of the mysterious creature that constitutes a woman; and with it the desire to be beautiful, to appeal, to feel in command through her own beauty. She was no longer as zealous of her child as previously, and she started to show more care for her own person. Her husband was pleased to see this change as, oddly enough, when he noticed her desperate devotion to her child and the house, he was glad at first, but when he saw the queen of his heart so shabbily dressed, pale and miserable, his heart was pierced and he wished once more for the enchanting fairy who sat languishing by the window, waiting for his return, and whose feet he worshipped. So strange is the human heart, and so much bitterness was left within him from the former days of chivalry, when woman served as an image of Saint Maria, and as a bed companion. But now there was something else as well. He had become quite tired and spoilt in his self-indulgent habits during his wife's first period of motherhood. He came and left with his hat on, ate off the corner of the table, and didn't always dress with much care. But now that his wife was starting to return to her old life and ways, he neglected to follow suit and amend his manners. His wife, who was of an unhealthy disposition, took these diminishing civilities to be an indication of a lack of love, and she had the additional misfortune of realising that she had made him depressed. What a sad day it was! The time was approaching when the payment would have to be made. There had been a good harvest, but even if it produced what it promised, not even the surplus would be able to cover everything; the knight had to find another way out, and he found one. He had fine carpentry timber felled around the grounds, but the felling came too close to the building, so that a lime tree that his wife was especially fond of was also chopped down. He hadn't done this out of spite, and in fact was unaware that it was his wife's own special lime tree. His wife had been lying ill for a few weeks, and when she now entered the hall she saw that the lime tree was missing. Her immediate thought was that it had been removed in order to cause her grief. But she could also see that her rose bushes had dried up as well; for no one had had the time to think about such trivialities during the rush to secure transport and equipment for the harvest. But she believed this had been done out of enmity towards her, and so she had all of the farm's draught animals sent to fetch some water.

'At this point a new circumstance arises that accelerates the onset of her unhappiness. The bailiff has moved into the castle in order to supervise the salvage of the harvest. He happens to be visiting the wife just after she has made the two discoveries. They find out that they are childhood friends, and they engage in heart-to-heart conversation, which grants her some distraction. She finds a certain pleasure in the visitor's coarse but courteous manners, and the comparisons she draws between the bailiff's politeness and her husband's clumsiness do not work in the husband's favour. For she forgets that her husband can also be just as polite during a morning visit, and that the bailiff can be just as impolite in everyday affairs.

'And so everything had been prepared for what would happen when the husband came home. The bailiff had gone, leaving the wife alone with her thoughts. When the husband comes in, he is pleased; firstly, to see his wife back on her feet and, secondly, because the long drought promises good weather for the salvaging of the harvest, as all of his crops have now been stooked, ready for gathering that day. But the wife, who is oppressed by her thoughts, feels wounded by her husband's contentment. And now the shots were fired, one by one. The wife asks about her lime tree. The husband explains that he had no wish to chop down that one in particular, that it was felled along with all the others. What about the roses? The husband replies that he never took it upon himself to water them. At that point the wife, who is at a loss for an answer, discovers that he has his outer boots on and immediately makes a remark about it. The husband acknowledges his misdemeanour and wants to make amends by taking off his boots straightaway, but then the wife becomes outraged at such a display of disrespect. Harsh words ensue, and the wife insists that her husband no longer loves her. The knight then replies roughly as follows: "You say I don't love you because I'm working for you and not sitting chatting by your sewing hoop; I don't love you because I'm hungry after going without food; I don't love you because I don't take my boots off when I enter a room for a moment; I don't love you, you say! Oh, if only you knew how much I love you." Then the wife replies more or less in this way: "Before we were married you loved me even though you were chatting by my sewing hoop, even though you took off your boots and even though you didn't show me contempt. What has happened since then, after you changed your behaviour?" The husband replies: "We got married!" The wife believes her husband considers that marriage has granted him possession of her, and that he wants to demonstrate this through his self-assured behaviour. But this assuredness can quite simply be explained by his unquestioning belief in her promises to love in desire and in need; by the fact that he believes in her indulgence while dispensing with a great many hollow ceremonies in order to avoid wasting time. He is close to telling her everything; that the reason why he works in the field, thinks about the fields, tramples on the soil and brings dirt into their home is to keep danger at bay. But he keeps silent for he cannot trust that she would now, as frail as she is, be able to bear the blow, and he knows that in a day or so everything will be over, and the house will be saved. He asks her to forgive him; and they forgive each other and exchange tender words again. And then the blow strikes! The butler rushes in and announces that a storm is approaching. The wife is glad that her roses will have rain, but not so the husband.

'The knight then feels the hand of the Lord upon him, and he tells his wife everything, but asks her not to lose hope. He issues an instruction for all the draught animals to be harnessed and then brought in straightaway. The animals are being used to fetch water, comes the reply. Who has sent them out? "I have," replies the wife. "I wanted some water for my flowers, which you allowed to dry out while I was sick." - "You're not ashamed to admit it?" asks the knight. And then out it comes: "You boast about having lied an entire year! I don't need to be ashamed of telling the truth, as I haven't done anything wrong, I have only been unfortunate enough to be the victim of a misadventure!" Then the husband becomes furious, walks up to her with his hand raised, and strikes her.'

'He was damn well right to do so,' said the count.

'Now, now, young Sir, to strike a weak woman!'

'Why not? If we hit children, why not women?'

'Because women are weaker, Sir.'

'All the more reason! If we stand no chance against the strong, and we can't strike the weak, who *can* we strike?'

'We must not strike anyone, my friend! The things you say, and to think you want to become a warrior in arms.'

'Yes, indeed! Isn't that what it's like in war? The stronger strike and the weaker are beaten. Isn't there logic in that?'

'Logic there may be, but there's no morality in it. But don't you want to hear how the story continues?'

'That's probably the end of it - of the love, at any rate!'

'Oh, no, Sir, not by a long way. Love doesn't go away all that quickly. Well, by now she was fully convinced, just like you, that their love had reached an end, and she asked the bailiff, who was due to arrive, to request in her name that the king grant her a divorce.'

'And she wanted to leave her child?'

'No, she intended to keep it. Her pride was wounded deeply, and she felt crushed under the great edifice of her dreams that was collapsing around her.'

'And what of her husband?'

'He was devastated! His dream of finding happiness in love was over. And he was ruined besides, as the floods from the rain had washed away and destroyed all his crops. And when he saw that she, whom he loved with all his soul, was the one who had caused his misfortune, he felt resentment towards her. But when his anger had abated, he found that he still loved her.'

'Still?'

'Yes, Sir. For love does not ask why. It only knows that that's how it is! Hard times followed. The knight was destroyed, and he abandoned his castle to wander aimlessly around the forests and fields on his horse. Mrs Margit, on the other hand, awoke to a life of power and activity, and took the management of the whole house in hand. Necessity had given so much strength to the small, fragile creature, who had never worked. She sewed clothes for herself and her child, she paid bills and took care of the farm workers - and this was not the easiest of tasks, as the workers had become accustomed to regarding the small, spoilt woman as a mere guest, but she dealt with them with a firm hand. And when the money ran out, she pawned off all of her jewellery, and with this supply of funds paid wages and debts. One day, when the knight had come to his senses and returned with trepidation to tend to the household affairs, which he believed to be beyond help, he found everything in good order, and after making enquiries, he was told that it was his wife who had salvaged everything. He becomes ashamed and remorseful. He goes to his wife, gets down on his knees and begs her to forgive him, admitting that he didn't know how to appreciate her before. She forgives him, and explains that she was not worthy of being held in higher esteem, as she did not possess the qualities she acquired later. They become reconciled as friends, but she declares that her love is dead and that she does not intend to remain his wife. The conversation is interrupted by the bailiff, who in the meantime has been living in the house and giving Mrs Margit advice and assistance. The husband feels he has been cast aside for another, and finds his position occupied. Jealousy rages within him and he forbids his wife to receive a strange man in his home. His wife explains that she'll accompany the bailiff to his room - at that point the husband becomes indignant and starts talking about his rights over her person since, by law, she was still his wife. But she has received the divorce decree that very morning and now declares that she is free to go wherever she pleases. Now that he sees it's all over, he falls down on his knees and begs her to stay. When she sees the proud knight crawling on the floor like a slave, she loses the last shred of respect she still harbours for him, and when she remembers how she, weak and wretched, once looked up to him as the one who would carry her in his arms over thorns and rocks, she wants to rid herself of this image, and when she can no longer find in him the man he once was for her, he ceases to exist and she leaves.'

'And so,' interrupted the count, who thought the story was becoming a little boring, 'that was the end of it!'

'No, no, young Sir. It only appeared to be - it was not the end yet! But here I have a confession to make. I saw everything with my own eyes, Sir, as I was her friend, and in my heart I worshipped her. I would also like to confess how foolish I was. We old folk, who were brought up when the age of chivalry was drawing to a close, we had learnt to see in a woman a being that was raised above the ordinary people. We admired her appearance, her beauty, her impractical side, and we perceived women as, above all, something pleasing to the eye. And you can imagine that I, who nevertheless sought the truth, became so bewildered by these old ideas that I thought she was sinking just as she had reached the pinnacle of her labours and toil. Yes, on the very day when the divorce decree arrived, I had a conversation with her that I still recall, as though I had written it down. What I said to her was something like this: "If only you knew how impiously aloft you once stood before me. And I saw the angel shed her white wings, I saw the fairy lose her golden shoes, I saw how the bluebird swapped its haven. I saw you the morning after the wedding, when you were chasing through the forest on your white horse. He carried you with such ease over the wet grass, he lifted you high above the mire of the marshes without leaving a single stain on the silvery veneer of your clothing. For a moment I thought as I stood behind the trees: what if she should fall! And the thought took on an image. I saw you in the marshes, the black water gushing over you, your golden hair spread like sunshine over the white flowers of the Myrica gale. You were sinking, sinking, until I could only see your little hand. Then I heard a falcon whistling high in the air, ascending into the sky on his wings, until he was hidden in the clouds!" But then she replied - and how right she was! - "You once said, a long time ago, that reality with its dust and dirt was given to us by God, and that we should not berate it but accept it for what it is. Well, now! You are now saying, in concealed words, that I have sunk, because I'm on the way to reconciling myself with this life. I have exchanged the attire of the rich for the clothes of the poor, because I am poor. I have lost my youth, I lost it when I fulfilled the laws of nature and became a mother. My hands have been ruined by the needle, my eyes by sorrow, I am oppressed by life's burdens. But my soul rises, it rises into the sky like the falcon, towards freedom, while my earthly body sinks into the mire amongst the stinking flowers".

'I then asked whether she really believed she would be able to keep her soul held high while her body sank. To that she replied - no! For, you see, she lived as I did, under the misapprehension that there was something that was sinking. But her body wasn't foundering under work, on the contrary, it was being hardened and strengthened, and then it became better. It rose, it didn't sink. But we were both so foolish as to imagine that, for that's how we had imagined it since our childhood, and therefore we regarded white hands, which were actually unhealthy, as more beautiful than those that had become callous and brown through hard work. That's how mad we were in my youth, Sir - and probably still are, here and there. But in my madness I managed to commit a crime. "Release the falcon and let it rise!" I said. "I've certainly thought of that," she replied, understanding my thoughts, "but the chain is strong." - "I have the key to it," I replied. She asked to be given it and I gave her a poison bottle. And here I return to the story where I left off. It was at this point that she left her husband's room to look for the bailiff in his rooms on the upper floor. When she went up, she had to wait, as he was receiving people. There she was was given an abrupt lesson, as some old married friends refused to greet her since she had dissolved her marriage. One of these friends had been unfaithful to her husband and had a lover but still considered herself too good to take Mrs Margit's hand. What is one to say to that? At the time, it was considered the worst of all crimes to dissolve a marriage, but now, thank God, we have different ideas. She had come, as I said, to seek the bailiff's advice and help, just as she had always done before whenever she was in difficulty. Did she love him? Probably not, but the heart is never so easily deceived as in such cases. She imagined she did, as she believed she had lost the other one, and she had not been born and raised to be alone. But the bailiff, he was a different type of man. By nature, he was one of those seraglio birds, and if he hadn't been so cowardly, he would have lured the knight's wife to him. But that's not what he did, for he saw that that fruit would surely enough fall into his lap just as soon as it ripened. Therefore, he waited. But he had another characteristic as well; he was as conceited as a cockerel in a hen house, and he believed himself to be a devil of a seducer, whom no woman could resist. Now that he could hear Mrs Margit's reply, that she intended to visit him in his room, he thought the horses had been harnessed and therefore prepared himself for the journey. And so he leaves his rooms in order to receive her, just as you would meet your girl for the first time. They meet and she doesn't suspect anything to start with, as she is counting on his friendship and devotion. She wants to talk about life's most profound gravity, which awaits her. He talks about his love, but she would rather not listen to that. She is free, but she still feels bound. The power of her memories hold her back, and perhaps her old love still has a say in the matter. He becomes bolder, and begs her on his knees for her love. She then feels contempt for him. His vanity is wounded and he forgets himself, reveals himself and becomes violent. I arrive by chance and manage to strike him the death blow by informing Mrs Margit that he is engaged to be married. He can do no other than to withdraw. But, with her last hope and her last dream crushed, she had already acquired the key to the gate of eternity. Knowing that the poison needed an hour to take effect, I seized the opportunity to speak with her, as you would speak with someone who was about to die. Oh, I was definitely the man to prepare a person for their death! But, you see, what's for certain is that love for this miserable life is strong, and at such moments it's as if the human soul is turned upside down in a vat, as if everything lying on the bottom comes to the top, all memories come to the surface, all old faith - however unreasonable it may be, and however sincerely we may have discarded it - it rises again, and out of her I shook her old convictions of duty, foolish perhaps, but now necessary. I managed to bring her to the point that she wished to live, to start again in a convent, in privation and reflection. I even got her to want to exchange this convent, which no longer existed, for home imprisonment, where there is penitence in mutual self-deprivation, where there is devotion in the fulfilment of duties, where there is cause to exercise duty and obedience. She fought her pride and regretted her confession. She raged against the life that had deceived her, against the people who had lied and said that life was a pleasure garden, that they would find absolute happiness in marriage, as otherwise there was no happiness in life at all. She raged on, but fate came to my aid. The child, whose room was situated below, started to cry. At that point she is shaken to the very core, and she wants to live in order to teach her child that life is not what people say it is, and she didn't want to abandon it to the very destiny that she herself had avoided. She didn't talk about her husband; whether she was thinking about him now, I cannot say. I, who had given her the poison, also knew where the antidote was, but I still wanted to keep her in suspense, and I gave her less hope than I had myself. I left.

'When I came back, I found her in her husband's arms. He had met her on the stairs, where she had collapsed in a stupor. All had been forgiven, and all had been forgotten. You find that strange! But haven't you forgiven your mother even though she has given you a flogging, and does your mother not love you even though you have lied to her, caused her grief and aggravation? The last shakings had turned her soul inside out, so that the old love had come to the top like a translucent pearl that had been fished up from the sea's muddy bed, where it had lain concealed in a dirty mollusc. But she was still fighting her pride and said that she didn't want to love him, although she did love him. I'll never forget his reply, in which the entire riddle was contained. "You didn't want to love me, Margit," he said, "for your pride forbade you, but you love me nevertheless. You love me, even though I raised my hand, even though I was shamefully cowardly when misfortune came. I wanted to hate you because you left me, I wanted to kill you because you wanted to sacrifice your child, and still I love you. Don't you believe, then, in love's power over our evil volition?"

'That's what he said, and now I say, as the fable's narrator: this fable teaches us that love is a great force that goes beyond our understanding, and in the face of which our will is capable of nothing. Love suffers everything, forgoes everything, and of faith, hope and love, Sir, love is the greatest.'

'Hmm, but what happened then?'

'Then I was no longer present.'

'They continued to argue?'

'I know that they have the occasional dispute, as that's what people do if they think differently, but I also know that neither wants to be master of the other, rather that they walk their path making fewer demands on life, and therefore they're as happy as one can be if one accepts life as it is. And this is precisely what the old age, which claimed to be able to create a heaven on earth, did not want, but what the new age is learning to do. And that is the end.'

The Last Shot

It was one of the last days of October in 1648, and the streets of the little town of Lindau am Bodensee were bustling with life. This Swabian Venice, floating on its three islets off the Bavarian shoreline, had for a long time been besieged by the Swedish field marshal Wrangel, who in recent years had been cooperating with the French, and now occupied a fortified and elevated position in the town of Eschach. The peace talks, which had been conducted for four years, had not brought about any ceasefire. On the contrary, Königsmarck had recently stormed Prague. Nevertheless, this event had accelerated the negotiations in Osnabrück and Münster, and allowed the rumours of an impending peace to travel as far south as Swabia.

For several months now, Lindau had suffered all the phases of the siege. On his return from an excursion to his home in Bregenz in the afternoon of that day, when the bombardments of recent days from Eschach had died down, the mayor paid a visit to the *Gasthof zur Krone*, since the Town Hall had been razed to the ground, to see if he could find an acquaintance who was not occupied on the bulwarks. No-one was to be found on the premises. Somewhat dejected, he stepped out onto the terrace to survey the town, to see what action the Swedes might be taking in their camp on the other shore.

The surface of Lake Constance was smooth and reflected the snowy peaks of Hohe Säntis above St Gallen. To the west, the edges of the Black Forest stood out smoky blue like an evening cloud, and to the south, the Rhine forked off between Vorarlberg and Rhätikon until its clay-yellow ripples merged with the turquoise waves of the lake. But the mayor had no eye for the beauty of nature, as for the last eight days he had been half-starved, and for more than a month had suffered the trials and hardships of battle. He just stood and observed how the affable Bavarian mingled with the ill-tempered Württemberger and the vivacious Badenser in the throngs scurrying along the Beach Road. He watched as people flocked to the Franciscan Church to receive the sacrament. Down on the shore he caught sight of a group who stood staring out into the lake, where some barrels appeared to be drifting towards them, carried along by the weak current. They were making eager attempts to haul them ashore with boat hooks and lines.

'What have you got there, good people?' called the mayor from the terrace.

'It's a gift from those kind-hearted Swiss in St Gallen!' came a voice in reply.

'Probably wine or liqueur which has been lying in wait for a westerly wind to bring it across from Romanshorn,' added another voice.

The mayor withdrew from the terrace and went inside the tavern to sit and wait to hear what the fishing on the shore had produced.

The corpulent Bavarian's seemingly motionless facial features expressed concern, anxiety and vexation. His huge fist, resting on the oaken table, opened and closed as he weighed up the options of either springing into action or holding back. He stamped his foot on the unswept floor - his toes almost pushing through the buckskin of his jackboot - which created a cloud of dust like smoke from a tobacco pipe. But he had no peace of mind. Presently he rested his broadsword against the floor, and out of his cordovan bag with a silver coat of arms he took out a couple of enormous keys, which he tried in an invisible keyhole, as if attempting to lock a door in such a way that it could never be opened again. He then brought the bunch of keys up to his mouth and uttered an appeal, one he had had ample time to learn during the long siege with its repelled attack, its failed sortie.

Loud steps on the stairs and the clatter of weapons made themselves immediately audible. In an instant, the mayor stuffed the keys back into the bag, slammed the clasp shut and threw the strap around his shoulders, so that the bag came to rest on his back. He then sat down with a posture that resembled a position of defence, as if he knew who was about to come through the door.

'May God's peace be with you, Major.' He greeted the officer entering, who slung his shabby top hat with its faded feather crest onto a bench.

'Welcome back, Mayor,' the major returned the greeting and sat down on the other side of the table.

A long silence ensued, as though both fighters had been loading their weapons to shoot each other down. Finally, the major broke the silence by asking brusquely:

'What did they say in Bregenz?'

'Not one sack of flour, not one beaker of wine will induce the town to hand over its keys!, they said.'

'Well?'

'Well?' repeated the mayor with a menacing look.

'You don't want to leave the keys?'

'No, a thousand times no, a million times no!' The mayor thundered and leapt up from his chair, his face blood-red.

'Do you know,' the major said, 'that all those corpses have brought nothing but pestilence to the town since the Swede took the cemetery in Eschach?'

'I know!'

'Do you know that all of the town's horses and dogs have been slaughtered?'

'I know! And I know that the first to lose his life was my own Packan, my companion for twenty years since I lost my wife and children!'

'Do you know that the lake has risen, so the cellars are full of water, which means that no-one can seek refuge in them should the bombardment continue.'

'I know!' replied the mayor.

'Do you know that our vines, standing on those hills over there at Hoierberg, Schachten and Eichbuhl, are ripe for harvesting, and that the Swede and the Frenchman have already made a swoop for the vineyards, like starlings?'

'I know! But do you know that peace could come to an end this very day, that perhaps it has already ended, and that we might salvage our honour if we defer capitulation for one more day.'

'One more day,' the major repeated. 'One more day! We've been saying that for three months, and in the meantime our children are dying. Perhaps you don't know that the cattle numbers have diminished since they've been eating moss on the roof, foliage from the trees, droppings from the stables, licking the millers' empty sacks, drinking their own urine! That's how it is, however, and now the children are crying for milk.'

'The children! Don't talk about children to me, someone whose own daughter was raped to death in front of her mother! At that time, I was the one begging for help, but what good did it do? Your problem was that you were unrepentant. To hell with the children! Why didn't you take them across the lake before the Swede put all his barges on the water!'

'A beast, that's what you are, Mayor, not a person! Perhaps you'd rather see them drowned in bags or eaten, as they were in Bohemia when Friedland was carrying on as he did!'

'Yes, we've been beasts amongst beasts for thirty years, with all this murder and fire and robbery and fornication. You could even call it war, as long as the Swedish king lived and led his soldiers. But then we've had arsonists and highwaymen, who plundered for the sake of plundering; Huns, Goths and Vandals, who destroyed out of anger that they were not able to produce…'

A cry from the street interrupted the major's reply and drew the disputing parties out onto the terrace. Huddled around the barrels that had just been hauled ashore, some draught animals appeared to be kicking in the bottoms of the vessels, so that the contents ran out onto the street.

'What's that you've got down there?' called the major.

'Oh, it's just milk, which those mean-spirited Swiss have sent us instead of wine,' came a reply from down below.

A woman carrying a child in her arms had walked up to the spot. When she saw the white stream on the street, she emitted the most terrible shrieks and placed her child down on the paving stones to let him drink. Lured by the screaming, several mothers soon gathered round and let their little ones lick up the sweet milk, like thirsty piglets, clinging to the paving slabs as if they were their mother's soft breast, while the mothers hurled curses at the brutish men who did not spare a thought for anyone other than themselves.

'Mr Mayor!' said the major, enraged by the odious scene, 'let's go up onto the roof, where we can see what the Swede is doing, and talk about our present situation! As you can see, people are at the end of their tether. What the one has no strength to hold onto the other one takes, families are on the verge of break-up, and the young are living in utter confusion; a riot can break out at any time.'

The mayor was not listening. He went up the stairs and crept out through a gap between the roof trusses onto the tiered ledges of the gabled wall. He then climbed further up to the pediment, which was crowned with a flag pole to which a telescope was attached. Beneath him the town revealed its total devastation. Not one intact roof could be seen. There was not a single tree left in the old plantations, which had been used for food and fuel. Towards the beach, all of the houses had been demolished, all gardens dug up to provide materials for bullet traps. The streets were full of shabby, hungry, dirty people behaving like savages, but all making their way towards the *Gasthof zur Krone*, which was already drawing flocks of people.

The mayor now put his eye to the spyglass, which he directed towards the beach. He saw hills, rising one above the other, with white croft houses underneath steep roofs and surrounded by plundered apple trees and patches of vineyards. In the middle of the hillside appeared Eschach with the Swedish headquarters. He could make out an unusual movement around the blue and yellow ensigns, and some cavalrymen appeared to be tending to the cannons, those the mayor had become familiar with during the long siege. He had even given names to the worst beasts in the rampart battery.

He had a long, spindly one of red copper, which had just smashed through the stained-glass windows of the town church and which he called *Red Dog*. To the left he had a crude mortar, which was given the name *The Thunder Bomb*, and this one was a regular scupper when it started to spurt out its contents. *The Devil's Mama* was the title he gave to a third, which was said to be of Swedish iron and the king's own invention. And so on and so forth. But behind the ramparts, on a garden terrace, he saw the field marshal sitting together with his officers and drinking *Seewein*, their wine, which they had cultivated, pressed and unwisely left in the cellars on the other beach. Over their glasses and pipes these high-ranking gentlemen were studying a drawing, which did not appear to be a map, however, and this reminded the mayor of a rumour that Wrangel had wanted to move the Bavarian palace of Aschaffenburg home to his estate by a lake up in Sweden, and when he realised this would not be possible, he instructed an architect to make drawings of the building, after emptying it first of furniture, household items and curios.

For an instant the sight of the wine and tobacco stirred the mayor's baser urges, which had been suppressed for so long, but his hatred and indignation, which had been nurtured for a lifetime, soon rose to the surface. For those who had no food or drink, who had lost everything they held dear and had no peace, the only thing left to them was their honour, and he had sworn on the death of his daughter, whom he himself had murdered so that she should not give birth to the devil's own offspring (a secret he could not offer up as a reason for his obstinacy), that he would not part with the keys to the city for as long as he lived.

He now watched as a puff of smoke was discharged from *Red Dog*. Then he heard something whining above his head, which then hit the ground with a bang on the Beach Road and was greeted with a loud cry.

'The keys, Mayor, or it's over for us!' the major shouted from the steps of the gabled wall below.

'To your positions, Major, on the ramparts, or you'll be hanged!' replied the mayor.

'Bring the keys here! Or we'll come and take them ourselves!' called the major.

'Come and get them!'

A mass of heads now appeared, crawling out through the attic window, and demanding in unison the keys to the city.

'Get down from the roof, they're aiming at us!' the mayor called out to the people, who were beginning to climb up onto the wall in order to carry out their threat.

In the next instant the flag pole was split apart like dry firewood and disappeared, the splinters following the shot, which dropped down through the ceiling.

The mayor turned half-way round, and would have fallen had he not supported himself with his great broadsword.

He righted himself and remained standing on the top-most slab like a steatite statue on a cathedral. The people, who had met their mayor's valiant conduct with a cry of enthusiasm, were once again driven by their determination to venture an attack on the person who held the keys to the city, without which a formal hand-over of the town was not considered possible.

With the support of the discontented public, the major attempted a final assault on the unyielding mayor. He therefore climbed up the hazardous staircase, drew his sword, and exhorted the mayor to either step down or defend himself where he was.

But it soon became apparent that his position was impregnable. Convinced that it would be impossible to get him to back down, the major turned to the mass of people and asked three times whether they would grant him the right to let the city gates be broken down and the white flag hoisted.

As his question was answered with tumultuous cries of assent, he turned round to leave the same way he had come and to make his way to the ramparts, followed by the crowds of people.

The mayor, who had now been left alone and realised that all hope of the town's salvation was lost, at first appeared to collapse, but got back up immediately afterwards, as if he had made a decision. With a trembling hand, he opened the bag, took out the large keys and, after making the sign of the cross, threw them as far out into the lake as he could. When they had disappeared into the deep, he fell on his knees and clasped his hands in long, silent prayer.

At this moment he wished he was deaf, but in his appeal to God and the holy virgin, he thought he could hear the blows of axes against the city gates, through which the enemy would enter to plunder and defile, hang and burn.

But after some time of silent prayer, he noticed that the silence had pervaded the whole town and the cannonade had ceased. From the ramparts only a faint murmur could be heard, as if people were talking at the same time. The murmur increased and became a rumble, which immediately afterwards broke out into cries of jubilation.

He got up from his kneeling position and saw a white flag flying high above the Swedish headquarters. Then a blow on a trumpet and a roll on a kettledrum could be heard, and were answered in like manner from Lindau's ramparts. And now the blows of the axes on the gates became audible. A boat set off from the Swedish headquarters. The field music played on the other beach, and a cry was carried through the town's streets; muffled at first, like the roar of the lakes against the cliffs, a noise without meaning, a cry without sense. But they were getting closer, and now he could make out the last word; *concluded*, although he did not know yet whether it referred to the capitulation or anything else.

Finally, the shouting became louder and clearer as the mass of people surged onto the Beach Road, tossing their hats and caps up at their courageous mayor: Peace is concluded!

*

'*Te Deum laudamus!*' were the words being sung in the Franciscan church in the evening, while the town's inhabitants became intoxicated on the barrels of wine which had been brought up from the beach.

And when the mass had finished, the mayor and the major were sitting over a jug of *Seewein* at the *Zur Krone*.

But the black shot that had brought down the flag pole and penetrated the ceiling could be seen through the joist in the middle of the room.

The mayor looked at the sphere on which shiny scratches gave it the semblance of a full moon breaking through the storm-driven clouds, and he smiled; he smiled for the first time in ten years. But then he broke down, as though he had done something evil.

'The last shot,' he said. 'A far cry from the first one in Prague, no more than a man's life span! And since then Bohemia has lost two of its three million people, and the Rhine-Palatinate is left with only a fiftieth of its inhabitants. Saxony has lost one million out of three, and Augsburg cannot count more than eighteen of its eighty thousand. And two years ago a hundred towns in our poor Bavaria went up in smoke and flames. Hessen is without seventeen towns, forty-seven palaces and four hundred villages. All for the sake of the Peace of Augsburg! For the Peace of Augsburg, Germany has been barbarised, butchered, rendered powerless and cut off from all seas, without a windpipe to the outside world, smothered, finished. *Finis Germaniæ.*'

'It most certainly was not the Peace of Augsburg that did it!' objected the major. 'Just listen to the Frenchman up there in the Swedish camp, the way he holds his masses like a good Catholic, and then tell me if it was Luther and the Pope who caused the war! No, it was surely something else!'

'Yes, it was definitely something else!' the mayor replied, emptied his glass and went home to sleep peacefully for the first time in thirty years - thirty long, dreadful years!

Printed in Great Britain
by Amazon